Sherlock Holmes

and the

Black Widower

by

Kieran E. McMullen

Paperback ISBN 9781780925073
ePub ISBN 978-1-78092-508-0
Mobipocket/Kindle ISBN 978-1-78092-509-7

Published in the UK by MX Publishing
335 Princess Park Manor, Royal Drive,
London, N11 3GX
www.mxpublishing.co.uk

Cover design by www.staunch.com

Dedicated

To Some of the best friends I've ever known:

Malarkey

Shorty

214

Horse

April

Jake

Red

and

Pepper

Contents

Chapter		Page

The Cast

Sherlock Holmes	Consulting Detective
John Watson	Physician
Mycroft Holmes	Government Official
Giles Lestrade	Inspector
Damon Mercer	Private Inquiry Agent
Colm Campbell	Nephew of Mrs Hudson
Lucy Ferrier	Watson's first wife
Mary Morstan	Watson's second wife
Lady Frances Carfax	Watson's third wife
Malalai	Afghan woman
Dick Smee	Taxi company owner
Biddy McGee	Maid
Colonel Ross	Horseman
Dr Anstruther	Friend of Watson
Dr Vincent Jackson	Friend of Watson
Theresa Heffernan	Cook

Arthur McMullen	Retired Colonel Indian Army
Liam Murray	Retired Orderly
Colonel Rowland	Retired British Army
Martha Hudson	Housekeeper

Sherlock Holmes

And the

Black Widower

By

Kieran E. McMullen

Princess Hotel

Pembroke, Bermuda

20 July 1929

My Dear Holmes,

I am enclosing the following manuscript more for your entertainment than edification. I believe you will find that it does not tell you anything you do not already know. However, it does lay out a precise history of events as I am able to remember them. Lacking the strength to pen it myself, I have told the tale to my friend Arthur, whom I'm sure you remember. He has been good enough to make sense of it and put it down. It has now been over 20 years since those days of turmoil, but I am proud to say that the events described did not affect our relationship. I always understood that you had a duty to investigate the allegations as brought to you by Lestrade.

I do not know if these events of 1908 belong in a published history of your cases. I leave that decision to you. I did feel the need over the last few months to write the story of the only time in our long relationship that you and I were at odds. I do not believe that I will long survive. The specialists have told me that I have mere weeks to live, if that. The cancer has progressed dramatically even in this wonderful climate. I expect to be taken to hospital this afternoon and there I will pass.

The one great memory of my life is my long association with you, my friend.

Do not be sad at my passing. Know that I am not. I wish you continued long life.

Your friend always,

John Watson

Chapter 1

The Keeping of Bees

The year 1903 was one of the first of the new century in which the world, for the most part, was at peace. The Boxers in China and the Boers in South Africa had been quieted by force. The rest of the world had been somewhat at peace. The Irish were making noise in Parliament as usual, Trans-Atlantic radio communication had been established, the Wright brothers made their world-changing powered flight in the States, and Thomas Edison had electrocuted an elephant named Topsy to prove the alternating current used by Westinghouse was far more dangerous than his direct current system. It was a tranquil year.

It was also the year of the retirement of Mr Sherlock Holmes, the world's first and may I say, finest, consulting detective. The year had started busily enough. There were adventures recorded and published by his friend, Dr John Watson, which he entitled *The Three Gables*, *The Mazarin Stone*, and *The Creeping*

Man. There was also the *Adventure of the Blanched Soldier* written by Holmes himself who, though he tried to avoid it, could not but fall into the use of drama in telling a tale of logical thinking. This was a fault that he constantly accused Watson of exhibiting.

It was October when Holmes moved to his retreat in Sussex. It was a beautiful place, a villa five miles from Eastbourne on the slopes of the Sussex Downs.

The house itself was fairly small. It consisted of a sitting room with fireplace and dining area, a large bedroom, a smaller bedroom and a kitchen, in the rear of the house was another small bedroom occupied by the housekeeper.

The cottage's thatched roof extended beyond the front door, thereby, making a type of veranda. From here, Holmes might sit in the evening with a clear view of the sea beyond. Here he spent many pleasant nights. He used a small table to hold a book or two or made notes of his study of bees. The cottage also boasted a few outbuildings, one for the storage of his bee-keeping and gardening equipment, the other an area to store the files of a life's work in detection.

It had taken Holmes over a year to find his retirement home, one that met all his desires. As anyone can tell you, bees do not like open areas for their hives. The salty winds coming from the sea would drive the creatures to a more sheltered place. Holmes had found the ideal location, for, to the rear of the house and but about a hundred yards away to the north beyond the outbuildings stood a copse of trees in a hollow. What an ideal shelter for the hives which Holmes had laid out in rows spaced about six feet apart.

To the north and west of the hives lay beef cattle and vegetable farms, to the east an apple orchard, and to the south the gentle upward sloping meadow which led to the cottage. It was a beekeeper's dream, at least, if not a bee's.

Holmes's entire household consisted of himself, Mrs Hudson, a dog named Ferdinand, and, of course, the bees. Ferdinand had been a gift from a politician upon Holmes's retirement about whom Dr Watson had promised to write someday, I believe he intended to call his story *The Adventure of the Politician, the Lighthouse and the Trained Cormorant.* Ferdinand was a fine example of a Border Collie, well trained and loyal. Finally there was the housekeeper, Martha Hudson, Holmes's former landlady and housekeeper at 221 Baker Street.

Mrs Hudson had been persuaded by Holmes to move to the countryside with him. She, as well as Dr Watson, was part of Holmes's natural surroundings. It was not an affair-de-coeur which brought Mrs Hudson to Sussex; it was the comfort of a familiar face and a good salary, though she had no real need of the money.

Mrs Hudson had been born Martha Grace Campbell to a middle class family in Londonderry. Her father, William Campbell, a bank manager and a good Scot Presbyterian, had married Carol Baron, a good Irish Catholic. Family life had forever been interesting in the political and religious arenas. But Martha was bright, pretty, the second girl, the third of five children, and cared for neither politics nor religious bickering. Born in 1857, she was only three years younger than her employer, a mere 46 years of age when she moved to Sussex, and still quite beautiful.

Martha had married Sergeant Malcolm Hudson of the Royal Horse Artillery in 1875. The couple were very happy. Sergeant Hudson was sent to the Curragh to train artillerymen for the next two years. William Patrick, their only son, was born there in 1877. But it was a sad year; outside the birth of their child, for Malcolm was re-joined to a battery and posted to South Africa. 1878 brought both bitter and glad news. Martha's aunt, one Martha Clark (nee Campbell), for whom the girl had been named, had died and left her a quite large and handsome house at 221 Baker Street in London.

She had visited her widowed aunt on numerous occasions as a girl and always marvelled at the size of the building. Martha wrote to Malcolm of their good fortune but wondered how they could ever afford to run such an immense house.

Taking Billy in tow, Martha went to London to try and decide what to do with her inheritance. She loved the house, but it was too large for her and one child and impossible to keep on a Sergeant's salary. "Perhaps," she wrote her sister Flora, "I could make it a boarding house. I shall write to Malcolm today and see what he says."

Before she could receive a reply to her letter, Martha was notified that she had become a widow. It was January 1879 and Malcolm had been killed by Zulus at some place called Isandhlwana along with a thousand other men. She was now alone with a small child and a large house. She would do everything she could to make a life for her and her son. She would be a landlady.

It was only two years later that Mr Sherlock Holmes and Dr John Watson came to rent rooms on the first floor of her boarding house. Martha was only 24 at the time and quite lovely in her own way. Her green eyes missed nothing as they supervised both the maid and the cook. She was thin, not over five foot six inches, and almost always wore a high collared grey day dress. She kept her auburn hair up at the back. She knew her place as landlady. She had always been conscious of class distinction. She did think the "good doctor" a handsome man, but would never dare to be forward. His friend Mr Holmes was pleasant enough, but quite eccentric. He came and went at all hours, had odd visitors, occasionally smelled up the house with horrible chemicals, and eventually would start shooting holes in the walls. That was the last straw!

At first, 221 Baker Street had been divided up such that the basement was kitchen and storage and a room for the cook. The ground floor was given over to offices and two small shops, one a tobacconist, the other a milliner. The first floor was divided into four suites to let, with two more on the second floor. Martha, Billy, and the maid also lived on the second floor.

Mr Holmes's eccentricities would eventually drive away most of the other lodgers. But as his fame grew, so did his remuneration to Mrs Hudson. In fact, with the income of the shop and office rentals and Mr Holmes' payments, Martha was quite well situated. She was frugal and made sure that young Billy learned the value of a penny. When he was old enough she made him a page boy and bought him a fine uniform jacket of blue and scarlet with brass buttons. Billy was proud of his uniform and worked hard to help his mother. He would stand next to the picture of his father in the uniform of the Royal Horse Artillery on the sideboard and ask Martha if he looked as good as "Da". Martha would put her money away and wait for better times to come.

But, as so often happens in a family, tragedy would strike twice. Billy enlisted in the Royal Horse when he was old enough and served in South Africa, like his father before him. And like his father before him, he did not return. In the same Second Boer War that took Holmes and Watson to South Africa[1], Billy died at Colenso while serving as a runner for Colonel Long, RHA.

So it was that upon Holmes's retirement (Watson had just been married for the third time), Martha decided to retire to the country as well. With her considerable savings and the sale of that most valuable property, she had no need of work; but it was what she knew and it was nice to have a purpose, even if it was to pick up after Sherlock Holmes.

---

[1] See *Sherlock Holmes and the Mystery of the Boer Wagon,* MX Publishing.

Chapter 2

A Proposal

Almost five years had passed since Holmes had moved to Sussex. They had been eventful years for the most part. Watson had lost his third wife, Mrs Hudson had lost her parents to death and two of her brothers had emigrated to Australia. Holmes had completed his treatise on bees and the world's governments were at each other's throats again.

In the mind of John Watson, May 1908 was to be a time of love and contentment. His third wife, the former Lady Frances Carfax, had died in 1904. Watson had then concentrated on his practice; feeling that perhaps his destiny in life was to be alone except for his friendship with Holmes. But of late his trips to the Sussex countryside had become more frequent. He had always thought Martha Hudson a fine looking woman, and Lord knows her patience had been boundless when it came to her most eccentric tenant, but he also found now that he had repressed feelings for the lady who had cooked and cleaned for him and Holmes over the years. In his heart, he knew he wanted her to be with him. After all, he was only 56 and she only 51. They were both still young. Well relatively, anyway. Perhaps she had feelings for him. This fine May Day he intended to find out for certain.

It was Ferdinand who drew Holmes's attention to Mr O'Brien's dog cart winding up the hill in the early morning haze.

"Well, friend Watson has gotten an early start today, has he not, boy?" asked Holmes, patting the dog on the head. Holmes rose from his chair and watched as Mr O'Brien's old mare ambled along the winding road below.

"We had best tell Mrs Hudson the good doctor is early and we will be in need of tea."

"The kettle is already on the boil, sir," came the gentle female brogue from the doorway of the house. Martha had not changed much in the last five years. Though the high-necked dresses had given way to a more country frock, the only other visible change had been a few shades of silver in the auburn hair which she now wore loosely.

"Mrs Hudson, had I your ability at premonition, I would have been as great a detective as our friend Dr Watson has claimed."

"You never were good at being humble, Mr Holmes," she smiled. "I'll away and get that tea. If Mr O'Brien sees me, he'll be talking of his carts and what a fine business he has."

"Yes," replied Homes. "He is sweet on you."

"Aye, sir, and I won't be leading him on."

Mrs Hudson retired inside as O'Brien's dog cart came around the corner of the house. Ferdinand ran back and forth in mad anticipation, for he knew that the man who came to visit always brought a treat, usually a bone, which needed to be chewed and carried and buried by the trees.

"Good day, Mr O'Brien," called Holmes, walking up to the cart. "Thank you for bringing Dr Watson from the station."

"My pleasure, Mr Holmes. I hope all is well here."

"Fine, Mr O'Brien," replied Holmes as Watson scrambled down from the high seat and grabbed his bag.

"And Mrs Hudson is well?" O'Brien appeared to be trying to see through the windows.

"Yes, I suspect she will be in the village later today."

"Will she now?" asked O'Brien with a grin. "Perhaps I'll see her there."

"Yes, perhaps."

"Thank You, Mr O'Brien," said Watson, handing the man a coin. "I've a noon train to catch tomorrow. Can you come back for me?"

"That I can do, Doctor. Well, say hello to Mrs Hudson for me." And with a tip of his cap O'Brien turned the mare about and headed back toward the village.

"Come, Watson, have a seat. You took an earlier train than usual. Not neglecting our patients, are we?"

Ferdinand was now running about the doctor in glee. Watson did not intend to disappoint. Putting his bag on the ground he extracted a small parcel wrapped in butcher paper. "Sit now, Ferdinand." The dog obeyed as Watson unwrapped a large bone and gave it to the animal. Ferdinand was gone in an instant. Such a treasure must be protected.

"You are spoiling my dog, sir."

"I just feel a kinship with the poor animal Holmes. After all, I know what it is like to live with you."

Both men smiled as they sat at the table on the veranda and Mrs Hudson appeared with the tea.

"How are you, Dr Watson? Good to see you again." She placed the tea tray on the table.

"Quite well, Mrs Hudson. You are looking well yourself. Holmes not being too much of a bother these days, I hope."

"No more than usual. At least he has his target practice outside these days." Martha smiled at Watson, hesitated a moment, and then excused herself. "I'll see to it you gentlemen have a proper lunch. I know you must be hungry already, doctor. I fancy you didn't take breakfast. No, now don't protest. You gentlemen enjoy your tea. I've things to do." Watson watched her as she walked back into the cottage.

"Well, Watson, shall I be mother?" Holmes picked up the teapot and started to pour.

"You have been visiting us fairly frequently of late," he continued. "This makes twice this month. Let's see, twice last month, and I believe three times the month before. The stationmaster must consider you a friend by now." He handed Watson a cup.

"Well, if it is too frequent, Holmes....."

"Not at all Watson, not at all, always happy to have you here." Holmes sipped at this tea. "I will admit things have been dull of late. It is good to have you about."

"Does Mycroft never visit, or is that a silly question?"

"No, I do get an occasional letter, of course. Even Inspector Jones and Chief Inspector Lestrade stop by from time to time for a little help."

"Does the Yard never tire of using your talents?" blustered Watson.

"Oh, I don't mind at all, Watson. Helps me stay sharp and keep my mind active, so to speak." Holmes put down his cup. "They have their reasons for coming, old boy, and you have yours."

"I?"

"Come, come, Watson. Your increase in visits hasn't been solely to talk of old times or days gone by. Even a blind man can see you are here to visit Mrs Hudson more than me."

"Holmes!"

"There is no point in denying it. She knows it as well as I do. Let's face it, you were meant to be married. Some men, like me, are not. You've been married, what, three times now isn't it? Widowered all three times, very unfortunate. But like the rider thrown from a bucking horse, you intend to ride again. I congratulate you, sir, on your determination."

Holmes leaned back in his chair to charge his pipe as Watson turned three shades of red. Rising from his chair he pointed a finger at Holmes.

"Holmes, that is, that is....well, true! So what of it?" He straightened his jacket as the wind left his sails.

"Sit, my friend. I am delighted for you. Our active campaigning has been done for a number of years now." Holmes drew on the pipe. "And if we have an occasional case, who would understand better you running off to the continent or wandering out in the night, pistol and jimmy bar in hand? No, I believe you should ask her. She has waited long enough."

Watson sat back down and looked out toward the sea. "You will miss her, Holmes, if she says yes. What of you?"

"Me? I shall get another housekeeper, of course,"

"Holmes, Holmes, Holmes," sighed Watson. "You know it will not be so easy."

16

"Perhaps not, but the happiness of my friends is more important."

Watson looked at Holmes and knew he was serious. Others had always been more important. He gave a good show, and he was self-centred enough but never to the detriment of others.

"I intend to ask her today, then."

Holmes studied his straight clay a moment.

"I need to check my hives, Watson." He rose. "You need not come with me. I know how the bees make you nervous. Make yourself comfortable and I'll be back in an hour or so." Holmes walked slowly around the corner of the cottage and disappeared from sight.

Watson sat for a moment watching the gulls circle by the cliff.

"Everything all right, Doctor?"

Mrs Hudson appeared, as if by magic, startling the daydreamer. "Mr Holmes gone to the hives, I suppose," she continued as she gathered up the tray. "There is plenty of water if you'd like more tea."

"No, oh no, I've had plenty, thank you." He stared at her; she was indeed a fine-looking woman. A woman who had shown great strength and great fortitude.

"Is something wrong, Doctor? You look as if you've something on your mind."

"Humph, sorry, I ah, well, do you think you can spare some moments? I should like to take a walk along the cliffs and company would be quite pleasant."

Mrs Hudson looked at him a moment in silence as if considering with great deliberation. "I should like that, Doctor," she murmured. "Let me get my shawl. It's windy up there."

She returned in a moment and the two walked up the slowly inclining path towards the cliffs. They were silent as they walked, each lost in his or her own thoughts. He trying to gather strength for the words he knew he wanted to say, she wondering if he would ask the question she had waited on for so many years. Would he finally ask?

As they stood on top of the cliffs the gulls swirled around them and a cool breeze came off the water, which somehow was both chilling and refreshing.

Watson looked at Martha, her auburn hair flittering in the breeze, her green eyes clear as she followed the path of a passing gull gliding below.

"Martha, we have known each other for many years now and I can't help but believe you know how much I admire you."

"Admiration is not enough, John," she replied before he could go on.

"Well, no," he sputtered. "But it's more, it's, it's…"

"Not very good with words for a writer, are you, Doctor?" She was smiling within. She'd waited half a lifetime for this. He was going to say the right words or she'd say no.

"Well, I mean." Watson looked at his hands which he noticed were shaking a bit. "Blast it, I love you, Martha. I have for years. You know I come here to see you more than Holmes." He fell silent a moment as he turned to her and held out his hand. "I have little to offer, Martha. I am a man of moderate means, but I can provide for you and more importantly I love you and want to be with you. Will you marry me?"

Martha looked at the extended hand, placing her own hand in his, she smiled at him.

"Of course, John. Could I say anything else? I have loved you, too, for many years. I would be proud to be your wife."

Watson pulled her close. As the two embraced, they kissed for the first time in the 28 years they had known each other.

They walked on the cliffs for a long time. They spoke of all the times past, of Billy, of their unspoken love over the years, and of the trials and thrills of sharing life with a character like Sherlock Holmes.

The "hardy" lunch was a bit late that day. It was well past noon when the newly engaged couple arrived back at the cottage arm-in-arm. Holmes was once again sitting on the veranda. As they came up the two steps Holmes rose from his chair.

"Congratulations, Watson," Holmes extended his hand to his friend, "and to you Mrs Hudson."

"Why, Mr Holmes, how did you..." started Mrs Hudson.

"An elementary deduction from the clues at hand," smiled Holmes and reaching out, embraced Mrs Hudson for the first and only time.

"And when is the wedding?" he continued. "I must have time to find a new housekeeper, after all." Holmes went back to the table to retrieve his pipe.

"We felt the fall would be good, perhaps late September." Watson looked at Martha for affirmation. Martha just smiled.

"Well, sir," replied Martha. "I believe I'd like to leave in August and go by my niece in London. That will still give you three months to find someone."

"You do leave me with a great problem, Mrs Hudson." Holmes drew on his pipe as he sat back down in his favourite chair.

"Well, sir, I'm sorry but I thought you would be quite happy for us." Martha was becoming upset.

"Oh, I am dear lady, but you still leave me with a great quandary. After all, where will I find another young lady of whom Mr O'Brien will approve?"

Martha hit him in the shoulder as she walked into the cottage, a smile on her face.

Chapter 3

A Visit from Lestrade

It was the first Saturday in June when Chief Inspector Lestrade came to visit Mr Holmes. He arrived at the mid-morning on Mr O'Brien's cart but he came without baggage. It was to be a short business meeting. It was a meeting that Lestrade was not eager to have and Mr Holmes was unaware of.

"Good morning to you, Inspector," called Mrs Hudson from the cottage door. "And to you, Mr O'Brien."

"Good morning, Mrs Hudson. Is Mr Holmes about?" Lestrade jumped down from the cart and started for the door before turning back to O'Brien. "Can you be back about two, Mr O'Brien? I must catch the late train."

"That I can, Chief Inspector, that I can. Good day, Mrs Hudson. Would you be needing anything from the village when I return?"

"Quite good of you to offer, Mr O'Brien but I think not, thank you."

"Until two then, Chief Inspector." With a click to his mare and a flick of the reins O'Brien turned the cart about.

"I understand congratulations are in order, Mrs Hudson," smiled Lestrade as he stepped up on the porch.

"I do thank you, sir." Mrs Hudson blushed a bit. "Some tea perhaps, sir? Mr Holmes is down at the hives but he should be back soon."

"That would be delightful if it would be no trouble."

"None at all. The kettle is already on awaiting Mr Holmes' return. Would you like a cup out here or in the kitchen?"

"The kitchen would do well, I'm sure. Make me feel at home. Lord knows I am there little enough these days." He followed as Mrs Hudson led the way into the kitchen. "I don't believe Mr O'Brien has given up hope, you know." Lestrade looked sideways at Mrs Hudson as she bent over the stove, a half-smile on his face.

"Mr O'Brien is a kind man, but I'm afraid he needs to look elsewhere, Chief Inspector. Cream?"

Lestrade sat at the table as she arranged the tea things.

"Thank you Mrs Hudson. Will you sit and join me?"

"I will that. I could use a cup. I must be in to the village shortly and do my shopping."

"Ah, soon you'll have someone to do that for you. You'll be the mistress of the house."

"That's as may be, sir, but I'll be wanting to do much myself. Habits of a lifetime are hard to break."

"That they are," agreed Lestrade. He seemed to be lost in thought a moment.

"Is everything alright, Mr Lestrade? Oh, I suppose you have a case on your mind. Come to ask Mr Holmes' advice I'm sure."

Lestrade straightened in his chair, "Yes, it is decidedly a strange one and I will be the first to admit not one I enjoy being involved in." He fell silent for a moment again and each looked at their tea cups. Mrs

Hudson would never pry, though her curiosity was strong.

"You know," continued Lestrade, "I retire in December. I've been on the force nearly forty years."

"My, I guess I should have known you'd been there quite a while, but somehow as days go by you lose track of time."

"In all those years, Mrs Hudson, I've never known finer men than the Doctor and Mr Holmes." He shifted his tea cup about aimlessly. "Oh, I know Holmes thinks I'm 'the best of a bad lot'. But he never treated me badly nor gave me bad advice. Course I didn't always listen." He smiled at the cup, "And the Doctor, well, he has never been anything but kind and generous, always a man to count on, like in that Baskerville business." Lestrade fell silent again.

"I don't know what your case is about, Chief Inspector," said Mrs Hudson, getting up from the table, "but I believe it is very personal and Mr Holmes will not fail you, I'm sure."

"Holmes has been known to fail on at least four occasions, Mrs Hudson," came a voice from the back doorway. The door was filled by the tall presence of Sherlock Holmes, Ferdinand at his side. "However, we try our best, do we not Chief Inspector?"

Holmes came to the table as Mrs Hudson set another cup.

"If you gentlemen will excuse me, I know you have a case of national importance to take care of. I, as women always do, will see to it that you get to eat while you save the world. I'm off to market. Sandwiches are on the sideboard, Mr Holmes."

Mrs Hudson crossed the room and gathered her shawl and basket. "Whatever it is, Chief Inspector, Mr Holmes will solve it." She patted Lestrade's shoulder as she left the cottage.

Ferdinand lay down by the cold fireplace as Holmes seated himself at the table and poured out a cup of tea. "Sandwich, Lestrade?"

"Perhaps later, Mr Holmes. I've come to see you on a very delicate matter. One that, even now I have come, I'm not sure I should address with you."

"Come, come. What has Mrs Hudson done? Stolen the crown jewels?"

Lestrade had been leaning back in his chair, balancing it on the two rear legs. At Holmes' words, he almost lost his balance.

"Blimey, Mr Holmes. How did you know?"

"So she has stolen the crown jewels?" smirked Holmes.

"No, of course not," Lestrade took a deep breath. "But how did you know it involved Mrs Hudson?"

"Quite simply by the fact that you avoided looking at her as she left."

Holmes pushed away the tea cup and looked intently at Lestrade.

"What is the problem? I cannot solve it unless I know what it is."

Lestrade looked straight into Holmes' face. "It is believed that Doctor Watson is a murderer."

Chapter 4

The Accusation

"What?!" cried Holmes. "How preposterous! He has shot men before, in battle or in a good cause, but a murderer? Who makes such an accusation?"

Lestrade stood up and started pacing back and forth across the small expanse of the room.

"It's like this, Mr Holmes," he said finally, stopping in front of the fireplace. "A gentleman named Colm Campbell went to the Commissioner. This Campbell fellow is a nephew of Mrs Hudson. I think he is the son of some brother of hers that lives in Australia or someplace. At any rate, he is concerned about his aunt marrying Dr Watson."

"Whatever for, my good man?" Holmes pushed back in his chair to look directly at Lestrade. "A finer gentleman couldn't be found. He has a good practice, a literary career, and he is a man of excellent character. What could be this nephew's objection and why come to the police? Please Lestrade, the facts."

Lestrade came back to the table and sat.

"It is the money, surely," continued Holmes. "Does he believe he will not inherit? Mrs Hudson does have a considerable savings I know. But she would not disinherit the boy. Watson doesn't need the money."

"That's just it, Mr Holmes." Lestrade, tragedy on his face looked at Holmes. "He says that Dr Watson is marrying his aunt for the money."

"Preposterous-- and if he were, there is no crime, just bad form," cried Holmes with a flick of his hand.

"But that's not the worst part, sir."

"Go on." Holmes was striking a match to light his pipe.

"This Campbell fellow claims that Watson marries for money and then, well, murders his wives."

Holmes sat, stunned, the match burning in his hand. As the flame touched his fingers he tossed the ember toward the floor and dropped the pipe on the table.

"And the Commissioner listens to this as if it were a serious accusation?"

"Yes, I know it sounds insane. I argued with Sir Melville for an hour about it but he has designs on higher office. He's a good man, Mr Holmes, but I believe that Colm Campbell is well connected and he has threatened to go to the press. It's just the kind of thing that old Horace Harker would love to get in the papers. If the accusation went public, think of the sensation, of the damage to Dr Watson. I'm afraid I ended by agreeing with Sir Melville. If it is to go public we had best be able to answer that we have investigated and there is nothing to it."

"Yes, of course, I see the point. What can I do to help? Were I to investigate this absurd allegation it would be considered useless. The public would say I found him innocent because he is my friend."

"True enough, but who knows him better than you? And you could give me all the information you gather. I will present the findings, not the details of how I gathered the information." Lestrade looked down at his hands. "Mr Holmes, for all our sakes, I need your help."

Holmes sat quietly for a while, looking at the empty fireplace. *How could anyone think, much less say, such a thing about Watson?*

"Yes, then, Lestrade. Give me the allegation precisely as it was made. What is this man's proof?"

"There is no real proof, just suspicion. But think of how it can be made to look. The doctor has been married three times, that we know of. Now, to lose one wife is unfortunate, two a tragedy, but three seems to be, well, suspicious."

"Perhaps. Continue."

"Each woman had an income or an inheritance so the Doctor profited monetarily from each death. He has his own income as well-- his pension, his practice and his writing. And yet..."

"Yes."

"He lives moderately. By now one would think him a wealthy man."

"Does a man have to live lavishly just because he has money? Look around you, Lestrade. I do not live so, yet I assure you I have funds to last well beyond my lifetime. This is ludicrous. What else have you?"

"Not much, I'm afraid, sir. I pulled out what was in the papers about each death. But I can't say I see anything there. His first wife died in a fall from a horse. Miss Mary, of course, had a heart attack while you were gone those three years, and Lady Frances died of tetanus."

"See there, Lestrade, three wives, three deaths, three dissimilar causes."

"The nephew will claim that while the first may have been an accident that the other two were preventable. After all, Watson is a doctor. Why didn't he save them?"

"It's all twaddle, Lestrade. You know it, Sir Melville knows it, and so do I. But I can understand where Campbell could cause quite a stir in the papers although I should think he would go to Langdale Pike, not Horace Harker, with his story."

"There was one more thing, Mr Holmes. Campbell claims that the doctor was married to a native girl in India. Now, I never heard about this, have you?"

Holmes stood up and walked to the fire. "No, Lestrade, that is just a story. I am familiar with Watson's time in India[2] and he was cordial with a young lady but she married another. So you see, this is all made of cod swaddle."

Holmes walked back to the table and retrieved his pipe.

---

[2] See *Watson's Afghan Adventure*, MX Publishing.

"I think I shall take a walk on the cliffs, Lestrade. No need to accompany me. Enjoy some of Mrs Hudson's sandwiches. Come, Ferdinand."

"Will you take the case, Mr Holmes?"

"Yes, Lestrade, I've no other choice. Do not miss your train. I will be in touch."

Holmes walked slowly from the door towards the cliffs. Ferdinand trotted alongside, tail held up, perhaps the man was taking him on an adventure or maybe for a treat.

It was an hour or two before sunset when Holmes and Ferdinand returned to the cottage. Lestrade had long gone and Mrs Hudson was in the midst of preparing dinner.

"I believe dinner will be delayed a bit, Mrs Hudson. I wish to go to the village and send a few telegrams."

"Alright, sir," sighed Mrs Hudson. *He's taken the case, whatever it is*, she thought. *No telling when meals will be.* "I'll just keep things warm until you return."

"Come, Ferdinand. It's only a mile across the hill. We shouldn't be more than an hour."

Holmes and the collie left Mrs Hudson to ponder when they would really return. He had messages to send. The first would be to Mycroft. If anyone could gather data on Watson's time in India, it would be he. The second telegram would be to Mercer, a private inquiry agent. He'd used Mercer on a number of occasions since his retirement. He would need an extra set of eyes and ears if he were to conclude this investigation, and Mercer was a fair substitute for Watson. Yes, he would have quite a bit of work for young Mercer.

Chapter 5

Research

It was well past dark when Holmes and Ferdinand returned to the cottage. Mrs Hudson was sitting in her rocking chair on the veranda darning socks by lamp light. She was rummaging through the housewife for more white thread when Holmes appeared at the gate.

"I'm afraid I had to take dinner off the stove, sir, or it would have been too dry. I'll warm it back up."

Holmes almost declined the offer, but thought better of it. "That would be excellent, Mrs Hudson. I believe I will have a brandy while you set the table. I have much to do tonight."

"It won't be long, sir. You just have a seat and I'll bring you your drink. Come, Ferdinand, time for your dinner, also."

Mrs Hudson went into the cottage, but Holmes was too caught up in his immediate concerns to sit down. First he must find his common place books. No, on second thought, he would do as Mrs Hudson suggested. He must clear his thoughts and decide on the exact line of inquiry to be taken. He would sit, smoke, and sip the brandy she had just set on the table. He must not let her suspect that his concerns were for her and Watson.

When the dinner plates had been cleared away, Holmes went to the bookcases on the far wall.

"Will there be anything else tonight, Mr Holmes?"

"No, Mrs Hudson. I will be doing some research tonight. I will take care of myself."

Martha smiled at the great man's back as he scoured the bookcases. She had been in her room a good two minutes before Holmes responded to her "good night."

One by one he found the books he was looking for, the obituaries of each of Doctor Watson's three wives: Lucy Ferrier, Mary Morstan, and Lady Frances Carfax.

Holmes had always found obituaries a mixed bag for information. While helpful as to the relationships, they were usually quite lacking as to cause of death. He found this only too true when it came to Watson's three wives.

"Died in a tragic horse accident, Lucy Watson (nee Ferrier) on 24 November 1887. Mrs Watson was an American born in the state of Kentucky. Being an orphan, she was raised by her grandfather..."

This was followed by more useless information about residence and being the wife of an up and coming author. It told Holmes nothing of which he needed to know, not even the location of the accident. He recalled it was on a hunt in the country, somewhere in Dartmoor, but where?

Holmes had been at their wedding in a small chapel in London upon Watson's return from California. Lucy was barely twenty and beautiful, slim, blonde hair, and the kindest of smiles. Watson had gone to California in response to a cry for help from his brother who had been completely disabled in an accident on the railroad where he was a construction engineer, as his father was before him. In order to live, while attending his brother, Watson had gone into practice in San Francisco. It was there that he met the beautiful Miss Lucy. When Watson's brother died, Watson brought the girl back to London and married her in early November of 1886. Just over a year later she was dead.

Holmes sighed. It seemed that was all he could remember. His habit of discarding from his memory any information for which he saw no purpose was now being counterproductive. He moved on to Mrs Watson number two.

"Mrs Mary Watson (nee Morstan), beloved wife of Dr John Watson (author of the Sherlock Holmes stories), died of a heart condition at their home in Kensington on 12 July. Mrs Watson was the daughter of the late Captain Arthur Morstan of the 34th Bombay Infantry. The couple had married in May of 1889 and lived most of their time in Paddington. Dr Watson, being a previous resident of Kensington, had re-purchased a former practice and only last month moved his wife to his old home."

Holmes pushed back into the soft cushion of his chair. *Let's see*, he thought, *that was 1892 when she died. They had been married for three years. She was a frail creature; Lord knows, she fainted twice just during the little business with the Agra treasure.* Holmes saw nothing suspicious there. *She, too, was an orphan, blonde, and what, nine maybe ten years younger than Watson. Well, one more to look at.* The sad time repeated itself in the third obituary.

The dateline was 5 August 1904. "This correspondent is sad to report the death of Lady Frances Carfax-Watson in Lausanne on the 31st of July past. Lady Frances, a well-known philanthropist, succumbed to a case of tetanus from an injury received in a carriage accident in Belgium. Lady Frances is survived by her husband, Dr John Watson, the renowned author. Services were held at the Church of the Nativity...."

No satisfaction there either. Holmes closed the book and rose from his chair. Ferdinand looked up from his place on the mat by the fire. Reaching for his tobacco-filled Persian slipper, he charged his pipe. He looked to the trusting face of the collie and smiled.

"Tell me, Ferdinand, what do you think?" He lighted the pipe and threw the match in the fireplace. "Three women, all very much similar in physique, mind you. All blonde, all about five foot four. All slim and pleasing to a man's eye, all younger than Watson. So we can accuse Watson of having a favourite physical type anyway." He sat back down and continued conversing with the collie. Ferdinand cocked his head to the right and gave every appearance of paying great attention.

"What else do we know, boy? Each had some money, no vast fortune, but they had no need to work or be taken care of. Let's see." He held up his hand and ticked each point off on his fingers. "Lucy had money from her grandfather who was killed in Utah, wasn't it? The dog panted in agreement. "Yes, I believe so. Mary, of course, had her six pearls from the Agra treasure, all quite valuable." Holmes ticked off a second finger. "Thirdly," he continued, "was Lady Frances. She had both income and the Spanish jewels. Those, you understand, were very valuable. Worth tens of thousands I would think.

"Are you getting all this, Ferdinand? You are looking as confused as Watson usually does. Now, on the other side, we have Watson. Doctor with a minor practice, a small wound pension, and one would think, a fair income from his writings. Oh, none of it is quite the quality of his friend Doyle with such things as his books on Professor Challenger, but the stories are published on both sides of the Atlantic. On the continent now, too, from what I understand. All of this is to the positive, I should say. Agreed?"

Ferdinand moved his head to the left.

"Yes, agreed then."

"On the negative side, we have what? Colm Campbell is suspicious. Watson, even with all these sources of income, must still work, and there is the old gambling problem, isn't there boy? It's been a long time since I kept his cheque book locked in my desk to keep him from betting on the horses."

Holmes got to his feet. "Come, boy, time to go to bed. We do not have enough data to posit any theory. Right now we only have our faith in the good doctor. I have said before that should a doctor turn his hand to crime, he is the first among criminals. He has nerve and he has knowledge. We must put aside our personal feeling for the good doctor and find the truth, whatever it may be."

Holmes was about to extinguish the lamp when Ferdinand came to his feet and rushed toward the front door, barking as he went. A moment later there came a hesitant knocking.

"Ferdinand, you be good, boy. It's only meself, O'Brien," called a familiar voice from the other side of the door.

Holmes placed a hand on the collie's head and opened the door. "Evening, Mr Holmes. Mr Barker asked if I wouldn't bring you this telegram, it was marked 'urgent', so I says I would."

"Very kind of you, Mr O'Brien. Would you care to come in a moment?"

"Is Mrs Hudson still up?"

"I'm afraid she is long to bed. It is well after midnight."

"Perhaps another time then, sir. Do you need to answer that?" O'Brien pointed at the paper in Holmes' hand.

"No, thank you, Mr O'Brien but I will be taking the first train to London in the morning. That is at half five, is it not?"

"Aye, sir. Should I send one of my boys with a cart?"

"No, I'll need the exercise. But I thank you for the offer. Good night, sir."

"Good night, Mr Holmes."

O'Brien left as Holmes re-read the telegram from Mercer.

Chapter 6

The Search Begins

The following morning Holmes was gone before Mrs Hudson arose. The note he left on the kitchen table was simple, "On Case". She fully understood he would be back whenever he was through.

Mercer was at the train station in London to meet Holmes. The trip had only taken two hours and it was still early. Mercer suggested coffee in the station's café and Holmes agreed.

Mercer had worked for Holmes on a number of occasions, most famously during the incident recorded as *"The Creeping Man."* He was of average height, about five foot eight inches, with brown hair, brown eyes, and a clean-shaven face. He always wore a bowler and a business suit. He was the type that fit in everywhere and that no one paid the least attention to. That made him perfect for a private inquiry agent. He had spent twenty years on the force before going off on his own. His contacts were many, inside and outside of the police department. He reminded Holmes of old Toby, the bloodhound. Put on a trail, he would not lose it.

They did not talk at all until the waitress had left coffee and scones on the table.

"Tell me what you have found out about the household," queried Holmes, as he stirred cream into the black mixture.

"Well, sir," replied Mercer, dipping his hand into his coat pocket to extract a small leather notebook. "I haven't had but a few hours since you contacted me and finding out information from twenty years ago is no easy task."

"Yes, I completely understand, but you have gleaned something or you wouldn't have taken out your notebook."

Mercer laughed. "Right you are, Mr Holmes, but it was that lead you gave me last night that made this part fairly easy. Not too many negro men are named 'Splayfoot Dick'."

"No, I should imagine that helped greatly. Have you located him?"

"Yes, sir. He goes by the name of Dick Smee. He is part-owner of a cab company here in London over on the West End. He and his partner have a fleet of hansom cabs and have started using automobiles also. Best I've gotten so far is that he came over from the States with Doctor Watson and his future wife, Miss Ferrier. There was also a maid, but I don't have anything on her yet."

"Right, I'll need you to find her. She was Irish, I believe, went to the U.S. and worked for Miss Ferrier and came back with her and Watson. Perhaps Splayfoot Dick can tell us where she is. Have you the address of the cab company?"

Mercer nodded as he gulped his coffee.

"Good, then let's see what Mr Smee has to say."

It was only a short ride by cab to the premises of Cunningham and Smee. The building was of a design that was probably not more than ten years old. It was brick, three stories tall with an interior yard. It ran half the block in length. The business office was on the northwest corner and it was here that the two detectives inquired for Mr Smee.

"He'll be on the first floor checking the horse stalls," replied a pretty secretary looking up from her typewriter.

"First floor?" replied Mercer.

"Yes, sir," she responded, "the cabs and automobiles are kept down here on the ground floor and the horses go up by a ramp in the back. Second floor is grain, hay, and harness." She had obviously explained all this before.

"And I suppose the central yard is to let in light on all floors," said Holmes.

"Yes, sir, all very modern. If you gentlemen will have a seat I'll send one of the boys for Mr Smee."

Holmes handed her his card, which she passed to a young boy who hastened out of the room.

Only four or five minutes passed before the door through which the boy had exited burst open.

"Mr Holmes! Mr Holmes! I declare but it has been a powerful long time since I seen you." Mercer knew that the man who entered could be none other than Splayfoot Dick.

He was a good looking gentleman of probably 60 years; though even Dick didn't know his real age. The American Civil War had freed him and his travels had taken him to Utah, where he became more a member of the Ferrier household, then just a hired hand. When the Mormons came after Mr Ferrier and Miss Lucy it was Dick, Miss Lucy's betrothed, Jefferson Hope, and a traveling salesman named Elias Fortescue Smee who helped the family fight their way out of the valley. Lucy's grandfather, John, had been killed outright and Jefferson Hope went over a mountain cliff in one of the running fights. It was Elias Smee who had seen the young girl to safety. Dick and a young Irish maid had kept the attackers busy at the homestead while the family escaped.

"Come into my office, sir. Sally girl," called Dick, "get my friends some coffee. The good kind, not that stuff what's been cookin' all mornin'."

Holmes and Mercer followed Dick into his office. It was spacious, well-appointed, and filled with bookcases. One wall was all windows from wainscoting to ceiling. It looked out on the interior yard, where men were moving carriages about and a blacksmith was shoeing horses. In the far corner of the yard, two men were working on an automobile.

"Sit, Mr Holmes, sit. It done been too long, I hope you're well. Does you ever see the Doctor?"

"Yes, Dick, now and then. This is an associate of mine, Mr Damon Mercer."

The men shook hands as Sally entered with a tray of coffee and started to pour.

"I see you lookin' at all dem books, Mr Holmes. Mr Smee taught me how valuable a book could be. I've never forgotten that or him. I read every chance I get. I took his name, you know. He was no relation to the Ferriers. He was just a fine man passin' through and he threw in wid us when he saw wrong being done. He's gone now but a finer man never lived. But what can I do for you?"

"First, sir, let me say how impressed I am at your success. You have done very well for yourself."

"Thank you, Mr Holmes, but part of that is because of Dr Watson."

Holmes looked at Mercer and back at Dick.

"I did not realize that. Just what did he do?"

"Well, sir, he told me never to tell, but seein' it's you." Dick moved his chair closed to the desk. "It was after Miss Lucy died. The Doctor was powerful sad, he moped about, didn't want to do nothin'. You saw how it was. Well, one day he comes to me and says, 'Dick, I know a man that needs a stable foreman. I can't be keepin you and Biddy on. Why, I have no work for you. What do you say?' Wasn't much to say. I took the job, worked hard, saved my money, and about ten years ago bought half the business. Doctor Watson helped me then too, put me with a banker what loaned

48

Cunningham and Smee the money to build this place. Fine man, the Doctor."

"I'm afraid I don't know the whole story of how you met the Doctor to begin with," said Holmes.

"Well, when Mr Smee and Miss Lucy escaped to California, them Mormons went after them. I snuck out of the valley and went to warn them. I hated leavin' Miss Biddy on her own, but she was a firestorm of a woman when she was riled. I figured she'd be alright and she was." He nodded aggressively at Mercer.

"Anyway," Dick continued, "they came after Miss Lucy. But Mr Hope, that was her beau, they thought he was dead but he weren't, just hurt real bad. Mr Hope killed them Mormons before he died, and he asked the Doctor to take care of Miss Lucy. That weren't no problem as the Doctor was already sweet on her." Dick leaned back in the leather chair. "She and Mr Smee and the Doctor, they all lived in the same boarding house.

"You probably know the rest, Mr Holmes. The Doctor, he brought Miss Lucy back here after his brother died. But Miss Lucy said 'I don't go unless Dick and Biddy comes too'. She even tried to get Mr Smee to come, but he wouldn't, said he had a whole country to see and books to sell. It was him though, that got Biddy outa' Utah, so she could come."

"What a great tale of adventure, Dick. I had no idea all this had happened. Doctor Watson is not one to speak of himself. But how did poor Lucy live, did Mr Smee sell books to pay the bills?"

"Oh no, Mr Holmes. Mr Smee had his own money but Miss Lucy had the gold her grandfather had hidden away in case the Mormons came after them. She also had the money Mr Hope had gotten from sellin' his cattle. No, she had plenty a money. She was always generous with me. So was the Doctor."

Holmes once again looked at Mercer. So it was true that Lucy Ferrier was a wealthy woman. Not rich by some standards, but well off.

"What happened to this Biddy?" asked Mercer.

"Biddy McGee was her name, sir, and I don't rightly know. I haven't seen her in quite some years. More coffee?"

Both men declined while Mercer scribbled in his notebook.

"I am trying to put together kind of a history of Doctor Watson's life, Dick. You understand, write a biography, sort of a return for all the stories he has written about me."

"Now ain't that fine!" smiled Dick.

"Yes, but one must tell of not only the triumphs but also the tragedies. Were you there when Miss Lucy had her unfortunate accident?"

Chapter 7

First Loss

Dick looked out the window. "I don't rightly like to think of that day, Mr Holmes. It was one of the saddest days of my life." Dick shook his head as if remembering were not the problem. The problem was forgetting.

"Mr Holmes, I'll tell you something. I never did understand that accident. I know if anybody does how ornery a horse can be. The very best rider can be thrown; the best cabby can have a run away. But still, when a rider like Miss Lucy gets killed like that, well, it ain't right. She could handle the most rambunctious horse I ever seen."

"Truly sad. Did she ride a lot when she came to England?" asked Holmes.

"All the time, all the time. Every time the doctor went off with you, she'd spend a whole day riding. She sure didn't like being left behind.

"Don't get me wrong Mr Holmes; she didn't mind the doctor going off to do some detection! She just wanted to go too."

"Sounds like she really loved the doctor," injected Mercer. "I mean to trust him to just wander off on some adventure."

"That she did, sir." Dick looked at his hands on the desk. "Course, he was always number two, if you understand me. Mr Hope, well, he was the love she'd never forget. But don't think that means anything. She loved the Doctor too."

"Exactly what happened, Mr Smee? I don't understand. Did she get thrown by a skittish horse?" Holmes let Mercer continue to press the issue while he observed.

Dick sighed. "We was out in Dartmoor at an estate. It belonged to some Army man who the Doctor knew. He was a darn good rider himself - the doctor that is - I don't know about the Colonel. That's what he was, a Colonel.

"Anyway, they was on one of them fox hunt stays. We'd been there about a week and everything seemed just dandy. Miss Lucy loved them hunts, ride like the wind she did. Well, it was a pretty day as I remember, November, the air was sweet and cool and them horses of the Doctor was feelin' good."

"The Doctor had horses at this Colonel's?"

"Oh yes, he had two or three that the Colonel kept for him."

Holmes eyed his fellow detective.

"Let Mr Smee continue, Mercer."

"At any rate, that mornin' the doctor and Miss Lucy got to arguin'. I know he never forgave himself for that. See, the Doctor didn't want her to ride Tawdry, that was the new mare. He thought the horse was too young and spooky for a hunt. Miss Lucy, she just poo-pooed the doctor. Wasn't no horse she couldn't ride."

"What did you think of the horse?" Mercer couldn't help himself.

"Young, not even three yet. She was quite a handful. I know I didn't want to ride her. Truth be known, I prefer mules." He almost whispered the last sentence as if he didn't want all the horses to hear. "She was a thoroughbred out of that race horse Somomy. Kind of a good match I thought, Lucy and her both head strong.

"As to the accident, I didn't see that, Mr Holmes. One of the Doctor's friends come running back to the stables yelling for a wagon and a gun. He said Miss Lucy was hurt so I didn't wait; I grabbed one of the horses and ran out where the man said. When I got there, Miss Lucy was already dead and that mare was back up on three legs. Her left front was broke clean in half down below the knee, and she was still crazy. Usual a horse hurt like that tries to move a bit but then stops cause of the pain. This horse kept jumpin' 'round. The Doctor's friend got back with the gun and gave it to the Doctor and he put that horse down. Course there was nothing else to do. Broke cannon bone like that ain't never goin' ta heal right."

"Did you ever hear how the accident happened?" asked Holmes.

"Seems that Miss Lucy was going over a gate and that mare started crow-hoppin' just as they got to it. Crashed through the gate, they did, and down into a gulch on the other side. Least Miss Lucy didn't suffer."

"Where was Doctor Watson?" It was Mercer's turn to ask questions.

"He was ridin' right in front a Miss Lucy so he didn't see her go down. He heard the crash of the horse going through and pulled up and come back. Lord, I felt sorry for that man." Dick shook his head again.

"You have been very helpful, Dick. I appreciate all you have told us." Holmes rose to go and Mercer followed. Both men came to shake hands with the entrepreneur. "One more thing: Did anyone examine the horse? I mean, was there any reason for her to suddenly act up?"

"No, sir; not that I know of. Course, I was busy tendin' to the Doctor and must say the tears was comin' down my face pretty good. There was one strange thing, though." Dick paused a moment before going on.

"Yes," prodded Holmes.

"Well, I've had to put enough horses down. I know how to do it proper. And the Doctor, he knew all 'bout them too. So when he shot that horse I couldn't rightly understand why he shot her where he did."

"Where do you shoot them?"

"They got a brain, Mr Holmes. Not like people, but they got one and if you make a line from left ear to right eye and right ear to left eye their brain is right where them lines cross. One shot and that poor animal goes down, no pain, no nothin'. But the Doctor, he takes that gun and he shoots that horse in one eye and then the other before he finds the brain. Three shots. But I guess he was so upset about Miss Lucy he didn't know what he was doin'!"

"I'm sure that was it." Holmes walked to the door as Dick came out from behind the desk.

"It was good seein' you again, Mr Holmes. Please come back some time. I'd like to show you our new automobiles."

"I would like that, Dick. Oh, would that estate in Dartmoor belong to a Colonel Ross?"

"That's it, Mr Holmes. How did you know?"

"Oh, I have had cause to deal with the gentleman in the past. Good day."

Leaving the stables of Cunningham and Smee, Holmes gave directions to Mercer.

"I want you to find this maid, Biddy McGee. I, in the meantime, will attempt to locate Colonel Ross and set up an appointment. I will be staying at the Langham Hotel. Send me a report tonight whether you make progress or not."

"You knew this Colonel Ross, sir?"

"I once had occasion to assist him in recovering a missing horse, named Silver Blaze. What I did not know was that he and Watson were friends."

Holmes turned on his heel and quickly marched away down the street.

"Until tonight," he called over his shoulder.

Mercer looked at his notebook and considered where to start his search for one Irish maid in a country full of Irish maids.

Chapter 8

Miss Biddy

Finding an address for Colonel Ross proved to be exceptionally easy. After checking in to the Langham Hotel, Holmes asked the clerk for their *Kelly's Post Office Directory*. Any good hotel kept a copy of *Kelly's*. The 3500 page book listed residential and commercial addresses of all kinds. Had he failed to find Ross' address in Kelly's, he would have moved on to *Who's Who* or the *Green Book of London Society*. As it was, he found what he was looking for in *Kelly's* and dispatched a telegram asking the Colonel for an appointment. Telephones had been in use for 30 years, but somehow Holmes just never liked them. There was something about talking to a person without seeing his face that he disliked. So many cues could be taken from a man's facial expression. The entire meaning of a sentence was changed not only by the tone of the voice but by the physical movement of the speaker.

It was late afternoon before Holmes received a reply to his telegram. Colonel Ross was on the Continent and not expected back until the following week. His secretary (whom Holmes remembered had been with the Colonel during the Silver Blaze affair) assured Holmes that the request would be passed on as soon as he returned.

Mercer, however, did not disappoint. That evening he met with Holmes. Mercer had followed a trail of half a dozen employers from over the years, finally locating Biddy McGee in Brighton.

"She is a housekeeping supervisor at the Grand Hotel," said Mercer as he lifted his whiskey. He and Holmes were seated in comfortable leather chairs in the smoking room, a small table between them.

"When can we talk to her?"

"Tomorrow, Mr Holmes. I've arranged with the management to make her available in the late morning." Mercer looked at his notebook. "It seems her name is now Coopersmith. She is married to a police sergeant, no children. The couple has an exemplary reputation." He put his notebook back in his breast pocket. "Should I go with you, sir?"

"No, I believe I will handle this myself. I have here a list of other people I would like you to find." Holmes passed a list to the detective. "I have one more thing I want you to work on. It will require exceptional delicacy; but I will wait a bit to give it to you."

Mercer returned a quizzical look and was about to say something but thought better of it.

"Now," continued Holmes, "please feel free to stay and enjoy your drink. I am going upstairs to my room. It is a short train ride to Brighton, but I wish to leave early."

Holmes was true to his promise of an early start. It was not yet nine in the morning as he stepped off the train at Brighton Station. The Grand Hotel being less than a mile and Holmes' appointment not for a few hours, he walked down Queen's Road to King's Road. But instead of turning right the two hundred paces to the hotel, he went left to the pier. The pier, with its' concessions and the beaches below, was always quite a study in humanity. It was just the start of the holiday season, so while many of the seasonal shops were now open, the crowds had not yet come. Holmes spent some time sitting on a bench at the end of the pier wondering about friend Watson. Finally seeing it was close to eleven o'clock, he walked briskly back to the Grand.

The desk clerk was quite helpful. Yes; Mr Holmes was expected. If he would care to wait in the assistant manager's office, Mrs Coopersmith would be sent right down. They were delighted to have such a notable person as himself visiting and tea would be sent in, compliments of the house.

Having shown Holmes into the office, the clerk disappeared, closing the door after making sure the tea was to his guest's liking.

The office was an interior one with no windows, a small desk, a couple of chairs, and shelves filled with files and account books. Judging by its orderliness, Holmes, felt sure the assistant manager was probably very competent. And if he were the one who suggested using this private office he also had some skill with people.

When the door re-opened in a few minutes, Holmes rose to greet Mrs Coopersmith. The woman appeared slightly nervous. She was rather short, no more than 5 foot 2 inches, mid-weight, brown hair, turning grey, and Holmes would estimate closer to 50 than 40. Her dark grey dress was clean and her apron starched and bright white. On her hair she wore a white cap, also starched. Her brown eyes were bright and her face showed a nervous crooked smile. The short fingernails and red cracks of her hands meant she was not afraid to work - just the kind of woman an hotel would like to have.

"Ah, good day. Mrs Coopersmith, is it?"

"Yes, sir. I was told to come here as there was a gentleman what needed to talk to me. Is that you, sir?"

"Yes, but please have a seat."

"No, thank you, sir. Now if you have a complaint about one of my girls, I …."

"Nothing of the kind, madam. You probably don't remember me; we've only met a couple of times. I am Doctor Watson's friend, Sherlock Holmes."

Biddy looked hard at the man. "Well, so it is. Faith, it's been many a year since I've seen you, or the Doctor for that matter. How is the Doctor? Well, I hope."

"Oh, yes; in fine shape. But please, have a seat."

"I venture I will, sir. Whatever brings you here? Holiday? Or are you following some criminal?" Biddy leaned forward and in a conspiratorial tone asked if he needed her to spy on a guest.

"Nothing like that, I assure you. I would like your help on something, though. It's for the good doctor."

"If there is anything I can do, I surely will, sir."

Holmes once again played out the story of wanting to do a history of Watson's life. Biddy was thrilled.

"I have much information about his time in America and your escape also from Utah, thanks to Mr Smee," Holmes said. "I also know much about the domestic arrangements once you all came here. What I do not have are the details of the tragedy that took Mrs Watson from us. I was hoping you could help."

"Ah, such tragedies, to lose two in one day like that." Biddy shook her head.

"You mean Miss Lucy and the horse?" Holmes was a little startled.

"I mean no such thing!" she replied with emphasis. "I mean her and the baby!"

Holmes was flabbergasted.

"I never knew she was pregnant," he replied quietly.

"No more did the Doctor until after the accident when they brought her back to the house. T'was I what had to tell him."

Watson never was very observant, thought Holmes.

"I take it she was not far along in the pregnancy."

"Only a couple, maybe three months, sir."

"How sad."

"Truly. And after all that the doctor takes time to make sure that me and Dick-- you remember him, no doubt-- that me and Dick are taken care of and get good positions. Just like that man. A saint he is. Well, most of the time."

"What do you mean, 'most of the time'?"

"Well, sir, it's like this, you know Miss Lucy was what you might call content. She loved the Doctor but it wasn't that passionate kind of love and I think he wanted that. But after Mr Hope died, it wasn't in her. The Doctor seemed to understand that. He had his practice and his horses."

"Did he own horses?"

"Oh, yes, sir, him and Mr Thurston, that friend of his what makes billiard tables. They had a couple of race horses and some to ride. Miss Lucy loved going to the Colonel's house and riding." Biddy started to tear. "She was so good at riding. That's what makes it all the stranger. She tried to cheer the Doctor up that day. He and the Colonel had been arguing something fierce about the Farmer's Fund."

"What is this Farmer's Fund?"

"I'm sure I don't really know, sir, but the Colonel wanted money for it and the Doctor said they were asking too much."

"What else do you remember about that day?"

"Far too much, sir. It was one of the saddest days of my life, but you don't need that. Besides arguing with the Colonel," she went on, "the Doctor argued with Miss Lucy about her riding that mare. He told her not to but she and Dick both thought it would be just fine."

"Tell me, Mrs Coopersmith, was Thurston on the hunt that day?"

"Oh my, yes, sir. He and the Doctor used to be in the front all the time. They both loved it. I asked the Doctor one time if you wouldn't like to come, but he said you wouldn't understand. I was never sure what he meant."

Holmes thanked the woman for her help and, after checking the ABC at the front desk, returned to the railway station to wait for the London train at two o'clock. First, he sent a telegram to Mercer adding one more name on the list of people to find - Thurston. Next, though, he must update Lestrade.

Chapter 9

In London

The train back to London gave Holmes the perfect opportunity to ponder what he had learned so far. Most importantly, it gave Holmes a chance to wonder about how little he really knew about Watson. He knew about Watson's time in Afghanistan, he knew of his competence as a surgeon[3], as a companion, and his wonderful gift for silence. What he hadn't known, nor appreciated, nor (to tell the truth) ever thought about was Watson's private life outside of their relationship. Race horses that he owned, a relationship with Colonel Ross that preceded the Silver Blaze affair, the loss of a child - he had known none of this. In truth, though, had he ever taken the time to know the details of Watson's life? The answer was a resounding no.

---

[3] See *Watson's Afghan Adventure*, MX Publishing.

Holmes had to admit that he had learned more about his companion in the last 72 hours than he had in the last 28 years.

Two of the telegrams Holmes had dispatched from the Brighton Railway station had been to Lestrade and Mycroft, asking both of them to meet with him at Mycroft's club, The Diogenes.

Mycroft, though seven years Sherlock's senior, was one of those public servants of the Crown who would never retire unless forced to. Like Sherlock, Mycroft was a bachelor whose work was his life. Mycroft's function in the King's government was quite unique. He was a clearing house of information. If the treasury needed to know the situation in a remote South American country or the Admiralty needed to know Russia's current status as to submarines, they went to Mycroft. His encyclopaedic knowledge, and more importantly, his ability to connect dissimilar actions made him invaluable. It was literally true that, at times, Mycroft *was* the British government.

It was close to five in the afternoon when Holmes arrived at the Diogenes Club. Lestrade was already in the "Strangers Room", the only room in the building where talking was allowed. Talking anywhere else was grounds for immediate dismissal from the club.

"Ah, Lestrade, good of you to come," said Holmes as he entered.

Lestrade had been standing, hands clasped behind his back, looking out the window to the street below. Mycroft was seated at a small writing desk, but rose when his brother entered.

"Good trip to Brighton, Sherlock?" inquired Mycroft.

"Yes and no."

"Hmm, well, dear brother, I have at least five different theories as to why you asked me to find out about a lost love of Doctor Watson's. I enumerated them to Lestrade but he has refused to 'confirm or deny' as the MP's say, any of my proposals. He wanted to await your arrival."

"Thought all that would be best coming from you, Mr Holmes." Lestrade was nervous and twisting the brim of his bowler in circles.

"Yes, well, have a seat brother Mycroft and I shall explain."

The three men sat around a deal table by the window. Lestrade kept his gaze out the window the entire time that Sherlock laid out the situation to Mycroft. When he had finished, there was silence for a moment. Mycroft was the first to speak.

"Obviously, a task such as this will take a bit of time. The intervening years have greatly added to the difficulty. Personally, I think it all sounds like twaddle and for this Campbell fellow to threaten to go public with gossip. I say let him. He can get a lesson like Oscar Wilde did."

"No, brother, we must do better than that for Watson." Holmes took a cigarette from his case and lighted it.

"I can see why your initial telegram to me was so sketchy, but I wish you had given me more to go on. I'm sure I did not ask all the right questions 'in my communiqué'."

"Whom have you been able to contact?

Mycroft took a paper off of the writing table.

"Watson's old orderly Murray is, as you said, in a place called Guthrie, Oklahoma." He looked over the top of his spectacles, "I understand it is a new American state." He looked back at the paper. "His old commander, Colonel Rowland is living in India and his former colleague Arthur McMullen is retired in Bermuda. Each is being contacted; as yet there are no replies."

Holmes turned to the Chief Inspector.

"Lestrade, I asked you to come so that I can keep you apprised of all my findings and all progress." He took a long pull on his cigarette. "Progress we have made a bit. Findings, we have none. As of this moment I have no reason to believe that the death of Lucy Watson was anything but an unfortunate accident. It is early, though, and I have at least two more people I wish to interview."

"I understand, Mr Holmes. What can I do? Surely there must be something?"

"Yes, Lestrade, I wish to know all there is to know about this Colm Campbell. Work habits, debts, any known or suspected criminal activity. Is he perhaps in some need of his inheritance or is all this truly just a concern for his aunt?"

"We don't usually investigate the complainant, Mr Holmes, but I think this is a special case. I'll see what I can do."

"And for me, Sherlock?" Mycroft sat and looked expectantly.

"For you, brother dear, nothing. I, however, intend to press on while friend Mercer locates Watson's billiard companion Thurston. I will look into the death of Mary Watson. I know that it happened while I was away in Tibet, but at least it is more recent than Lucy's death.

I would think that Watson's next door neighbour, Doctor Jackson, is still nearby, if not still in practice."

"Oh, he is, Mr Holmes. He still lives in the same house." The brothers looked at Lestrade. "My sister-in-law and her husband use him as their family physician."

"Excellent. There was a cook by the name of Heffernan whom I helped for Doctor Watson on a small matter. I never even had to meet the woman. Simple problem, I just told Watson it was obvious the woman's sister was at fault, but no matter. Can you find out if she is still about? I know she was there when I went on my little three-year journey."

"I'm sure we can find her. Is there anything else?"

"Not at the moment, Lestrade. Thank you for coming. I promise I will keep you posted as best I can."

"If there is nothing else gentlemen, I shall say goodnight," Lestrade picked up his bowler and hastened through the door.

When Lestrade had left, Mycroft broke the silence.

"So it goes neither one way nor the other."

"It is the problem of trying to prove a negative, Mycroft. All indications are that Lucy died in an accident, but I have learned so many new things about Watson that it makes me uneasy." Holmes lit another cigarette.

"Did he profit at Lucy's death? The answer is 'yes', by a trifle in pounds sterling, but at what cost? The life of a young woman and a child? Am I really to believe he did not know Lucy was pregnant?" he sighed. "It is possible."

Chapter 10

Mary

Mycroft rang for another brandy as he sat back at the writing desk.

"What did you not tell me in front of Lestrade, Sherlock?"

"Nothing, I'm afraid, Mycroft. I have nothing that points toward murder, but I will recount my actions in detail and perhaps you will see something."

Holmes laid out his movements and discussions while Mycroft leaned back, his eyes closed, and nodded at a point here and there. When Holmes had finished, his brother merely rubbed his chin.

"As you say, Sherlock, as it is, there is nothing. Next is Mary you said?"

"Yes, though we are not yet through with Miss Lucy."

"I am fairly familiar with the story Watson called *'The Sign of Four'*. It is greatly romanticized, but then the poor doctor was in love when he wrote it.

"True," Holmes smiled, "but that was Watson's usual state, depending on the lady at hand."

"As I remember," continued Mycroft, "the girl received six valuable pearls over a period of six years from an anonymous donor. Correct me if I err.

"One day she receives a letter that she is a wronged woman and she enlists your assistance to go to a meeting with one of the two sons of... who was it?"

"Major Sholto."

"Yes, yes. The first brother thought Mary deserving of a share of the great Agra treasure, which they had found after their father's death and just as their father ordered them to do. The other brother did not want to share. When you went to see the second brother, you found him dead and the treasure gone." He stopped to take a sip of his brandy. "You then tracked down the culprit, named Small, wasn't he? Yes, and his accomplice. You recovered an empty box, Small having thrown the treasure in the Thames. That about it? Oh, and Watson got the girl." Mycroft chuckled at his own cleverness.

"You do have an ability to skip over the details, but yes it was largely as you say."

"Largely?"

"As I recall, there were at least three incidents which occurred during the adventure which will be highly significant in our current case."

"Of course, you were there, so you are ahead of me, little brother. Those three things would be?"

"Firstly, that Captain Morstan, the man that Major Sholto cheated, his former subordinate, died of a heart attack; which shows a family weakness. Second, that Mary Morstan inherited her father's weakness as evidenced by her seemingly constant fainting spells. Well, perhaps not constant, but they occurred on several occasions." Holmes drew on his cigarette.

"And thirdly?" prompted Mycroft.

"Thirdly, that Watson had been alone with the treasure, or at least the empty box. Or should I say the box we assumed to be empty?"

"When was this?"

"You may remember from Watson's vivid tale that we chased the murderer Small, another man whom the Major had cheated, and his native friend Tonga down the Thames and finally caught him. Tonga was killed and the strong box with the treasure recovered. Watson wanted to take the treasure back to show Miss Morstan. Inspector Jones agreed to let him. We were not able to look at the treasure before Watson left because Small had thrown the key to the strongbox in the river. We put Watson off the chase launch at Vauxhall Bridge and he, along with one of Jones' subordinates, went to see Miss Morstan."

It was Holmes' turn to drink some brandy. "When they arrived at Mrs Forrester's home, where Mary was employed; Watson convinced the officer to wait in the cab while he showed the treasure to Mary."

"Ah, I see the difficulty. Was the treasure removed by Watson or by Watson and Miss Morstan and secreted in the house of Mrs Forrester?"

"Exactly," sighed Holmes. "Now, Watson specifically states that he broke open the lock to the strongbox with a poker and the box was empty. I, for one, do not doubt it. But how much better it would have been if the officer or Mrs Forrester had been present! As it was, Mrs Forrester was out for the evening."

The brothers sat in silence for some minutes.

"But see here, Sherlock, didn't Small say he threw the treasure in the river? That should exonerate the good doctor."

"That he did, yes. But consider, Small had no real quarrel with Miss Morstan, despite his statement to the contrary. After all, Captain Morstan had been cheated by Major Sholto, just as he had been.

"And why discard the treasure in the river, keep the box, and throw away the key? I understand not throwing the treasure complete into the river for the box might be found with its contents intact. But once the treasure had been scattered, why not throw the empty box and key in?"

"If Watson had the treasure, why would Small not tell?" countered Mycroft.

"Because he was going to the gallows for murdering one of the Sholto brothers and at least this way, one of those cheated by the Major would benefit."

"Yes, you could twist all the facts to fit that way. But I cannot believe that Watson would..."

"Nor can I, dear brother. Had he only not left the constable behind in the cab!"

"Yes, unfortunate. I'm afraid, dear boy, that I must be getting over to the Admiralty Offices. There seems to be some question about providing funds to White Star for some three large steamers that could be used as auxiliary cruisers. I really must go. I wish you better luck than you have had so far."

Mycroft moved toward the door as he continued.

"Consider, Sherlock, would the six pearls not have provided enough funds for Watson to buy that practice in Paddington? It could not have been too costly, it was not large."

"Yes, I'm sure it would have been."

"And tomorrow you will visit Paddington and see what is there. You will then go to Kensington to where the Watsons moved just before Mary's death. You will find there is nothing to all this." Mycroft started to close the door as he breathed the words, "I hope."

Chapter 11

Kensington

Holmes decided that Kensington would be his next destination, and the best time would be, as usual, a morning visit. Dr Jackson would most likely be on his rounds and Mrs Jackson and the servants would be more cooperative. After all, a doctor is most hesitant to give out information about his patients and the habit has a tendency to spill over to other things as well. He would talk to the doctor later.

True to his hope, he found upon calling at Dr Jackson's home and surgery the doctor was out.

"Might I speak to Mrs Jackson, then?" Holmes inquired of the young lady who had received him at the door.

"I'll see if she is in, sir. Would you wait in the parlour?"

Holmes looked about at a comfortable house. Well appointed, tidy, but with much bric-a-brac, as it was called. *This household has no children*, he thought, *never did*.

The girl returned in a moment and asked if Holmes would join her mistress out in the garden. He was escorted through a large living area and out a set of French doors to what he felt must have been the classic English garden. In the centre of the garden was a large wooden bench next to which stood a woman in work dress, heavy canvas gloves, and a large straw hat tied with a red ribbon.

"Forgive me for interfering with your gardening chores, Mrs Jackson. I do hope this is not too inconvenient a time."

"I am so delighted to meet you, Mr Holmes. We never had the pleasure when the Watsons lived here. How wonderful of you to stop by! I've asked Gladys for some tea in the summer house. Please, come this way."

Mrs Jackson led the way around to the back of the house, where a small gazebo stood in the centre of a quartering of flowering plants.

"How delightful," Holmes waxed enthusiastically.

"Oh, I'm so happy you think so, Mr Holmes. I'm afraid gardening is my passion. It always makes me feel young and vital when one looks at the blooms of nature." She looked about for a moment, enthralled by the bright colours. "Ah, here is our tea. We can sit and you can tell me to what I owe the honour of this visit. Vincent will be so sorry he missed you."

Holmes sat as Gladys poured the tea. Once the young woman had left, he again addressed Mrs Jackson.

"I have come in the hope of gaining knowledge, madam."

"From me?" Mrs Jackson seemed taken aback.

"Yes. You see, Dr Watson has, over the years, done me the great favour of writing about me. I am now in the throes of writing about him."

"Oh, how wonderful! But what has that to do with me?"

"Well, you see, madam, over the years, Dr Watson has taken it into his head to enter the married state several times." Holmes smiled and Mrs Jackson giggled. "So there are some periods of his life that I am not as familiar with as perhaps I should be because there were separations in our friendship. I come to you to help me correct that problem."

"Well I'm sure I'll tell you what I can, Mr Holmes, but the Doctor and his first wife, Lucy, kept much to themselves or were gone much of the time. I'm afraid English gardening was not really of interest to her. She was more the hunt set type, so we didn't see much of each other."

"What of Mary? I know they lived in Paddington at first but they moved back here, did they not?"

"Now, Mr Holmes, you are playing with me. You know very well they did." She tapped Holmes on the arm. "Oh, but then you were out of the country at that time, weren't you?"

"Yes. I'm afraid I was gone for a few years."

"Well, I'm not the one to talk, of course, but let's see. The Doctor and Mary moved here about two, maybe three, months before the tragedy. Oh, Vincent was delighted to have John buy his old practice back. The two of them got on so well, you know, and John was always willing to fill in if Vincent needed a day off." Mrs Jackson leaned closer. "And he didn't try to steal patients like a certain other doctor who bought the practice." She leaned back again. "And Mary, what a delightful young lady! So interested in the garden and quite willing to listen to advice and learn how to do things properly."

"Mrs Watson had other interests?"

"Perhaps, but she was such a nice homebody. I helped her greatly with the garden. It had quite gone to seed and she was bringing it back so wonderfully. She was quite getting the hang of it. You know, Mr Holmes, flowers, vegetables, shrubs, herbs, grasses. They all work together. It is really so exciting."

Holmes decided to just let Mrs Jackson talk. He would steer the conversation but not control it.

"So, Mary was interested?"

"Oh, my yes, and such a quick study. Of course, she was much more into flowers than anything else. How she loved the colours! And they moved here in the spring, just at the right time, you know."

"What were her favourite flowers?"

"Oh, I'm sure I don't know, Mr Holmes. I'm not sure that she knew. She was so excited about everything. Now, let's see, she had lupine, phlox, dianthus, foxglove, marigolds, pansies, candy tufts, and, of course, roses. She planted three or four varieties of roses."

Holmes froze for a moment. The significance of Mrs Jackson's remarks was not lost on him.

"Were you here on the day that Mrs Watson passed?"

"Oh yes, poor dear. Ellie found her, our cook. You can see over there" - she pointed toward the garden fence - "that the fence is just a little picket affair. It separated our vegetables from the Watsons' flowers. Well, Ellie had gone out to pick some early asparagus when she saw Mary just lying there. She came running back in calling for my husband, the doctor, you know."

Holmes smiled to himself.

"Well, Vincent came right away, but the poor dear was already gone."

"Where was Dr Watson?"

"Oh, he had left on his rounds. It was, oh, I don't know, two hours maybe three, before we were able to find him. I will never forget that day, it was horrible." Mrs Jackson shivered.

"Mr Holmes, what brings you here, sir?" Dr Jackson was approaching from the house, hand outstretched. Holmes rose to greet him. "You don't look ill," smiled the doctor. "Good to see you. Sit down, sir. It's nice to have a visitor who isn't coughing."

"Mr Holmes is writing a book about Dr Watson, dear," started his wife. "We were talking about poor Mary."

"Ah, yes, that was sad. Heart attack, you know. Right there in the garden. Such a nice lady."

"She had a weak heart, then?"

"Oh yes, John and I discussed it a number of times. He was very concerned about it. He wanted to be sure I knew about it if he was ever gone and something happened." Jackson poured himself some tea. "Wish I could have done something, but she was almost gone when Ellie found her."

"I understood she was already dead when the cook found her."

"Ellie? I'm surprised if she can even tell when the potatoes are done! No, the poor woman was still alive. Her maid and groom helped me get her in the house." He stirred in the sugar. "Died a few minutes later."

"Since I am not a physician myself, perhaps you can tell me what kind of signs you were looking at."

"Oh, she had the usual signs - dizziness, weakness, sweating, nausea, rapid heartbeat. Poor woman expired as we put her on the couch in the parlour. Sad indeed. Anyway, more tea? No?"

Holmes determined that the next stop he made would be the reading room of the British Museum to confirm what he already knew.

"I am afraid I must go in a moment, Doctor. Other matters also press upon me. But let me ask: Did Watson usually do rounds of a morning such as you do?"

"Oh, my, yes, quite usual. I had been delayed by a patient coming to the surgery that morning in need of stitches or I would have been gone already also. We had quite a time finding John. He had picked that very day to vary his route by starting where he usually ended. Sad, sad." Jackson shook his head again.

"And he sold the practice not long after?"

"Well, he was offered a good price and he could use the money, as I understood. He never said anything, but I just sensed there were money worries. He spent too much time writing, I think, not enough time on his practice. And he did like to go to the track, loved the horses. Went with him a few times. Very prudent bettor John was. Looked the horses over, checked on the jockeys and never put but a few quid on any horse. Very prudent. Did well too, on occasion."

Holmes thanked his hosts and left with a promise to visit again if he were in Kensington. His first stop would be the telegraph office, then on to the British Museum.

Chapter 12

Colonel Ross

Holmes only spent enough time at the British Museum, one of his old hunting grounds, to confirm what he already knew from Mrs Jackson. By late afternoon, he was back in the smoking room at the Langham Hotel waiting on Mercer. It was nearly five o'clock when his colleague finally appeared, and he proved to be without the information Holmes was waiting for.

"I'm afraid what you have asked for is going to be a little more difficult than we had hoped. The bankers really are steady about not disclosing information. However..." Mercer paused.

"You need funds to loosen some tongues, do you not?"

"Exactly, Mr Holmes. I'm sorry, but you know how it is: A few quid will make things slide a lot easier."

"Go by my bank in the morning. I will notify them that you are to be able to draw what you need up to £1,000. Will that do?"

"More than plenty, sir. I did have some better luck with the publishing house and the *Strand* magazine. Seems the Doctor gets paid quarterly on his books and a flat fee for each story. He keeps the rights and sells to the same stories to *Collier*'s magazine or whoever in the States. Then they bundle them up as a book and sell them again.

"I bought one of the *Strand*'s accountants a few pints and he made me a copy of the Doctor's account from last quarter. Here it is." Mercer passed a folded sheet to Holmes. "Nice penny, I tell you. I'd retire if I was making that kind of money. No late night babies for me."

Holmes looked at the paper and put it in his pocket. "Any luck on Thurston?"

"He's not in town, Mr Holmes. He's visiting friends in Scotland. Do you want me to find him there or wait until he comes back?"

Holmes considered a moment. "Wait, Mercer. We are already talking to too many people close to the doctor. He must find out what we are doing sooner or later, but later would be better."

"Are you Mr Holmes, sir?" A page was standing next to the table with a telegram on a salver in his hand.

Holmes took the paper from the boy and dropped a coin on the plate. The boy grinned. "Will there be an answer, sir?"

Holmes passed the communication to Mercer. "Yes, give me your pad."

Mercer waited until Holmes had answered the cable and dismissed the boy with an additional coin.

"Going to see the Colonel tomorrow?"

"Yes. As you see, he is back a few days early and can spare me some time tomorrow afternoon. For now, continue as you are doing. Come see me again tomorrow. And now, if you will excuse me, I believe I will catch the performance of Misch Elman, the Russian violinist. He is but 16 years old and already a great master. Good night, Mercer."

~ ~ ~ ~ ~ ~ ~ ~

The next day, the early afternoon found Holmes in a Cunningham and Smee taxicab on the way to the London townhome of Colonel Alonzo Ross, DSO, sportsman, big game hunter, and race horse enthusiast.

The ruse of writing a book was sure to fail with such a man. Holmes would be straight forward, to a point.

Holmes asked the cab driver to wait. After ringing the bell, he was shown into a brightly lighted morning room. He waited but a moment before Colonel Ross was wheeled into the room by a male orderly. The Colonel was now quite an old man, in his late eighties, surely. His hands were distorted by arthritis and a wool blanket draped his legs. He still had a full head of grey hair, however, and eyes that were bright and alert.

"Good afternoon, Colonel. You are looking rather well."

"I'll take that compliment, even when I know it is completely untrue," smiled the Colonel.

The two men shook hands and the Colonel asked the orderly to close the door on his way out.

"Leave the sherry tray here on the table before you go, Thompson. Good lad."

The "lad" must have been sixty but that would still make him more than twenty years the Colonel's junior.

"Well, Holmes, it's been what - seventeen, eighteen years since you helped me with that little affair of Silver Blaze? Haven't seen you since. Good piece of work that, though you worried me to the last minute. Sherry? No? The more for me then."

"It's the hip, I take it?"

"What? Ah, yes. Doctors tell me it will never be right again. No more riding for me." He stopped in mid-pour. "But…"

"The way you lean in the chair to relieve the pressure. No trick, I assure you."

"Well you haven't come to see me after all these years to talk of old times. What can I do for you, Mr Holmes? I am still in your debt."

"Colonel, I am involved in a case of the most delicate nature. It involves my friend Dr Watson. You remember him, of course."

"Certainly. We were quite close for a time. That is, until the death of his wife."

"Lucy?"

"Yes. He was a member of our hunt, up until then. He came out occasionally afterward, but, what can I say? He wasn't as strong about it as he used to be. Saw a good deal of him at the track. But what is this all about?"

"Sir, I must ask for your complete discretion on this matter. Not one word must leave this room, not to Watson, not to anyone."

"If you need my word as a gentleman, of course you have it."

"There has been an allegation of foul play in the death some twenty years ago of Lucy Watson."

"Astounding! Ridiculous! Twenty years later? What scoundrel makes such a claim?"

"That is of no consequence, sir. What I need to know is everything you can tell me about that day. Do you remember it?"

"Of course, sir. I'm not senile yet, just gamey." The Colonel downed his sherry. "As I remember, it was a beautiful fall day. Horse, a mare I believe, got away from Mrs Watson and the two of them crashed through a gate and down into a donga. Killed her, lamed the mare and Watson shot her. The mare, not his wife, of course."

"I understand that you and Dr Watson had had an argument that morning."

"Had we?"

"Something about a farmer's fund."

The Colonel thought for a moment. "I believe you are right, Mr Holmes, but it was not at all unusual to have that discussion with Watson. He always felt we paid the farmers too much. You would have thought he was short of funds all the time."

"What is this farmer's fund?"

"Not into hunting, are you? No. Well, it's nothing more than a payment the club makes to local farmers to keep them from making changes to their property that would hurt the hunt. For example, we ask them not to build gates higher than four rails so the horses can go over them. The same for fences. Don't want them too high. And you can imagine what barbed wire, like they use in America, would do to a horse."

"I see, yes. You mentioned that you saw Watson at the track frequently?"

"Yes, especially once he started investing in race horses."

"Did he invest heavily?"

"Mr Holmes, you astound me. Surely you know that your friend owned a piece of many horses over the years! Why, he owned ten per cent of Silver Blaze."

Holmes was again taken back.

"No, sir, I did not know that."

"I thought that that was the reason you agreed to take the case."

"I am afraid, Colonel, that I am learning many things I never knew about Watson. One last question. Did he and Mrs Watson appear to get along?"

"Indeed, sir. I never saw a more loving couple."

Holmes left the Colonel to his sherry and returned to the Langham. How little he had really known Watson. How much he had taken him for granted. Of course, Watson had never been part of the puzzle before. Or, rather, had never been the suspect - and that now made him far more interesting!

Chapter 13

Stalemate

As he approached the desk at the Langham, Holmes was interrupted by Lestrade and another man. The stranger appeared to be 25 years of age, tall, dark hair and eyes, and a flat nose. He wore the suit of a prosperous business man, but he did not wear it well.

"Excuse me, Mr Holmes," started Lestrade, "but this is..."

"Mr Colm Campbell, of course. May I speak with you alone, Lestrade? Excuse us, sir."

"Now wait here, Mr Holmes." piped in Campbell with a flick of his hand. "You don't get to just brush me off like that. Sir Melville says I'm to be told what's going on and I intend to find out! Tell him, Inspector."

Holmes had never seen Lestrade in a fit of rage. He had seen the police official confused, dejected, and inspired, but never like this. Lestrade's face was crimson and he seemed about to explode. Breathing deeply, he put a hand up in front of Campbell.

"Mr Holmes is a civilian, Mr Campbell, and neither Sir Melville nor anyone else can make him talk to you if he does not desire. If you will wait here a moment, I will be right back."

Holmes put a hand on Lestrade's shoulder. "It's all right, Chief Inspector. Obviously, Sir Melville has become aware of my asking questions. As to you, Mr Campbell, I have nothing I wish to say to you or to the police at this time. Should that situation change, I assure you that, whatever I discover will be shared with the proper authorities. If they wish to inform you, that is their business."

"We shall see about that, Mr Holmes!" Campbell cried in a loud voice. The assembled guests in the foyer watched a stormy departure.

"So, Lestrade, shall we sit in the smoking room for a moment?"

"Thank you, sir. I could use a bit of a relax. That toff is a little big for his britches, I think."

The two detectives found seats at a table near the windows and sat quietly for a few minutes.

"I take it you still have nothing to report, Mr Holmes?"

"How did Sir Melville find out I was on the case?"

"I'm afraid that's my fault, Mr Holmes. I was talking with Gregson and didn't tell him not to say anything. I'm dreadfully sorry."

"Well, it really doesn't matter. To answer your first question, no. There is no evidence that Watson murdered anyone." Holmes slowly took his cigarette case from his breast pocket. "But, there is also no evidence that he did not. We are still in a stalemate and that, of course, goes to Watson."

"How much more is there to do?"

"Quite a bit, my friend. We're fairly started but there is much more." Holmes lighted his cigarette. "It seems there is a side to Watson that I never knew."

Lestrade looked at Holmes a minute, question on his tongue, but again he chose not to speak. The two sat in silence.

"You want to ask me something, Lestrade. What is it?"

"It's about the gambling. Now, I know the Doctor liked the ponies and I've been able to make some inquiries at his club, the Army-Navy. Oh, I haven't talked to the members, of course, just to some of those what work there."

"Very wise, Lestrade. No one knows more about what goes on in a household or a club than the servants. They are always a wealth of information. And what did you find out?"

"It seems the Doctor didn't just bet on ponies. He bet on billiard games and rugby matches and almost any sporting event. Never much, you understand. Wilkins, he's the major-domo, says he never saw Watson pass up a bet but he can't remember anything more than a few bob on anything."

"Yes, as you say. Watson liked to wager. There was a time, I confess, when I had to keep his cheque book locked in my desk or he would have bet his wound pension. However, as has just been affirmed, he gives every appearance of having controlled his addiction. Ah, I see my man, Mercer." Holmes waved a hand to catch Mercer's eye and the detective hastened to the table.

"Lestrade, you know Mercer, do you not?"

"We were mates years ago when he was with the force," responded Lestrade. "How are you, Damon?"

The two detectives shook hands and Mercer pulled up a chair.

"Ready to retire, I hear, Giles. 'Bout time to spend some time with the grandchildren, isn't it?"

"Not if you knew my grandchildren," quipped Lestrade. "I'm better off dealing with the coshers."

Evidently the two men had stayed friends though Mercer had gone his separate way.

"Have you anything for me?" Holmes was still not one for small talk.

"No, sir. But I hope to have something for you by tomorrow night."

"That reminds me, I almost forgot, Mr Holmes." Lestrade rummaged in his pockets until he found a piece of paper. "Here it is, Theresa Heffernan, cook, lives over in Stepney. Here's the address."

Holmes took his watch from his pocket. "Does she work at this address?"

"Lives there, too. Has a little room on the ground floor next to the kitchen." Lestrade took out his watch also. "And now, gentlemen, since my official duty day is over, may I be permitted to buy you each a drink?"

Mercer agreed instantly. Holmes hesitated a moment, but seeing Lestrade's desire to be compatriots and not just associates, he also agreed.

"Tomorrow will be soon enough to see Miss Heffernan. Have you found anything out about our friend Mr Campbell?"

"That I have, Mr Holmes, though not much." Lestrade rummaged through his pockets once again until he found a bit of paper. "We knew he was a banker, but seems he's worse than that, he's a solicitor. Unmarried, has an flat in Soho, no club or church affiliation, and no close friends that we can find. Not well liked at work either, quite the loner."

"And his finances?"

"Now that was a little tricky but he is more than well off. Must have saved every penny he has ever made." Lestrade returned the paper to his pocket.

"No vices, no hobbies?" Holmes was very interested in a man with so sterile a life.

Lestrade grinned and took a drink before he spoke. "He plays the ponies!"

Chapter 14

The Cook

Stepney was not the best of districts, but not the worst. The address Lestrade had been given proved to be next to St. Dunstan's Church, where lays the tomb of Sir Thomas Spert. The building to which Holmes went appeared to be a mission for sailors and travellers who came from the dock areas on the north side of the river.

It was not yet nine of the morning, but the mission building was active with men, mostly older, and perhaps finding it difficult to find a berth on ships plying the seas from the Thames.

There was a large room filled with tables and chairs, at some of which sat poor souls nursing a cup of tea. At the far end of the room was a serving line, now vacant except for a large copper pot and a rack of cups.

Beyond the serving line Holmes could see a kitchen in which three women hustled about, cleaning and scouring.

"Excuse me, madam," Holmes said to a lady of grey hair and large frame. "I am looking for Miss Theresa Heffernan. I understand she works here."

"That she does, mate," replied the woman with a toothless smile. She wiped her hands on the apron she wore. "Over there by the sinks. Come to give her her inheritance?" cackled the creature. "Solicitor you look like, dearie."

Holmes smiled; he still had the ability to put everyone at ease.

"No, madam, the King just needs me to ask her a question."

The old woman roared with laughter and went back to her stove.

"Miss Heffernan, is it?" inquired Holmes.

A woman of about thirty-five, short black hair, slight of build and with a pleasant round face, turned to greet Holmes.

"Yes, sir. What can I do for you?"

"Is there someplace we can talk? I am Sherlock Holmes. You do not know me, I'm sure, but I have a few questions to ask you about your former employer, Dr John Watson."

"We never met, but I know you all right, sir. Dr Watson used to talk about you ever so much." Her dark eyes actually sparkled when she mentioned Watson. "We have a little room over here where we take our breaks. You go get a seat, sir, and I'll get some tea. About time for a cup anyway."

Holmes entered a small cubby hole of a room off to the side of the kitchen. The room contained but a wooden table and several small chairs. The walls were lined with shelves full of boxed and canned goods. In a moment Theresa entered with a metal tray on which sat two thick cups of tea. She took the next few minutes fixing the contents of the cups. When she had finally seated herself, Holmes sat across from her.

"I understand that you live here, Miss Heffernan."

"Yes, sir. I have a room on the other side of the kitchen... Just a bit of a room, but it does me nicely. But what of Dr Watson, he is all right, isn't he?"

Holmes explained about his book project. The woman seemed delighted.

"Oh, whatever I can do, Mr Holmes. Dr Watson was very kind to me. He's the one that got me set up here."

The puzzled look on Holmes' face must have shown, for the woman laughed and placed her hand to her mouth.

"You thought I just worked here, didn't you? Well, I expected a better deduction from Sherlock Holmes," she giggled. "No, sir. This is my mission. I run it. Oh, I rent the building from the church, and I work hard for donations to continue, but I set it up with some money Dr Watson gave me after his poor wife died." She took a sip of the tea.

"Had to let me go, you know. But I was a good cook and he knew what I really wanted to do. So he got the money to get me started. I dearly love that man. But I'm taking up your time, sir, what was it you wanted to ask me?"

"You were there the day Mrs Watson, that is Mary Watson, died?"

"That I was sir. Tragic it was. She was out in her garden. Loved that garden, she did. We hadn't been there long. I came with them when they moved from Paddington, but she was really making a go of it."

"It's too bad the doctor had already left on his rounds. He might have been able to do something."

"Oh, he wasn't on his rounds, sir. He was over at the shooting club. That's why Mr Clark, he was the groom, couldn't find him at first. We all thought he was on rounds, but when Mr Clark couldn't find him, he started checking places the Doctor liked to go."

"What was this shooting club you mentioned?"

"Silly, isn't it? Men, I mean. Spending a whole day with a gun, shooting at birds made out of clay. It's not like you can eat them. But the Doctor enjoyed it, went quite a bit he did. Liked to stay active."

"Did Mrs Watson not like to go?"

"Oh, I'm sure it wasn't permitted, sir. Besides, she was always a little sickly. Doctor said her heart wasn't good. Gave her some kind of medicine to help her. I think she felt quite left out at times, if you know what I mean. She didn't seem to mind the doctor running off with you here and there on an adventure, but it was lonely for her. I felt kind of sorry for her."

Theresa stirred the little bit of tea that remained in her cup.

"I think they weren't as well matched as they thought they were at first, Mr Holmes. Him the

adventurous type and her being the home person."
Theresa sighed, "to each his own, though. I don't know
what else I can tell you, Mr Holmes. Both the Doctor
and Mrs Watson were just good people to work for."

"Just a couple more questions, if you please."
Holmes paused. "Do you remember the name of the
medicine that Mrs Watson used to take?"

"Oh, I really couldn't say, sir, I'm sure. It was so
long ago."

"Was it digitalis?"

"Maybe, but as I said, I don't remember, if I
ever knew."

"And lastly, did the doctor pay well?"

Theresa seemed taken aback. "No better nor
worse than most, sir, I'm sure."

"So it surprised you when he offered to help
you open the mission?"

"Oh, yes. Quite a surprise. But wasn't that just
like him? He always did for others. Such a kind man."

Holmes thanked the woman and decided to
walk and think for a while. Watson was nothing if not
filled with contradictions.

It is time to have Watson to dinner, thought Holmes as he strode off briskly down the street.

Chapter 15

Dinner with the Suspect

Holmes's dinner invitation did not go unheeded. Watson, always one for good fare, met the detective at Simpson's-on-the-Strand promptly at eight. The dinner would be exceptional as always and the conversation varied. The topics included their mutual friend Winston Churchill, with whom they had served in the Boer War, the upcoming election (Holmes had no idea as to the candidates), the on-going Olympics (England had taken up the task when Rome had to cancel due to volcanic eruptions) and the Irish-Americans who refused to dip the American flag when passing the King's reviewing stand. Eventually, after some fine beef, and now over cognac, the subject of the upcoming nuptials had to arise.

"Have you advertised for a housekeeper?" asked Watson with a smile.

"Not yet good fellow. There is yet time, and of course, she may change her mind. Women have been known to do that, you know." Holmes looked at his friend with a devilish grin as he tapped his cigar ash.

"Oh, no, you won't get my goat," laughed Watson. "I know her better than that."

"Now, dear fellow, I hate to say it, but you may be meant to live alone. You have had three tragedies in your life, or is it four? No, three surely."

Watson looked down at the table cloth. "You are correct there, my friend." He shook his head. "I wonder why? I've loved each of them, Holmes. Why should each have been taken from me? It does make one wonder.

"Of course I have been fortunate, too. I have been able each time to not only lose myself in my writing and my practice, but in some fearsome adventures with my best friend. Your re-appearance in '94 from your three year journey made a tremendous difference in my life. I shall never forget it."

"You were doing wonderfully, old man. I know the death of Mary was a horrible experience." Holmes signalled the waiter for two more cognacs.

"It is interesting," he continued, "how each one was taken in a different way. A riding accident, a heart attack, and Lady Frances was tetanus, was it not?"

"Yes, and worst of all Holmes, each was preventable or curable and I, a doctor, and unable to save them."

"But a horse accident, Watson! No one can predict such things. The creatures react to the most trivial annoyances at times. But the horse Lucy was riding, she was unfamiliar with it or it balked at the wrong time or something." Holmes watched his friend intently through half closed eyes that seemed to peer at the ceiling.

"Yes, a mare. I was slightly familiar with it and asked her not to ride it but she insisted. It balked at the gate and she went down with Lucy. It gave me no pleasure to destroy the horse, but no pain either."

"A blind eye perhaps that had gone unnoticed?"

Watson seemed to hesitate, his hand slowly tapping ash into the tray.

"I don't believe so, no. And I have known many horses that rode well with one blind eye."

"See, it was no fault of yours. And Mary's heart attack. We both knew she had inherited the weakness from her father. It was something that could have happened at any time. You were out on rounds or something, were you not? How could you predict such a thing?"

"True, I was gone that morning. In fact, it was several hours later that I was told. When I returned to the house, Dr Jackson had already seen to what could be done."

"Had she been on medication of any kind?"

"Yes, digitalis."

"Again, Watson, you seem to blame yourself for something you could not control. And Lady Frances was again out of your ability to prevent."

"Now there, Holmes, I am not so sure. The tetanus toxoid should have worked. Why it did not, I do not understand."

Watson sat back and blew smoke into the air.

"Of course," he went on, "her constitution was weak after her near-death by being buried alive by those fiends. She was still on the path to recovery when we had the accident in Belgium. I'm afraid modern medicine has much to learn yet."

"Do you ever visit their graves?"

"No, I do not. I'm afraid I'm one of those that feels when the body is buried it is best to move on. Anyway, Frances wished to be cremated and her ashes spread across Lake Geneva." A glassy look came into the doctor's eyes as if he were about to tear. "She did love Lake Geneva so."

The friends sat for a moment, each lost in thought.

"But come, Holmes," brightened Watson, pulling himself up in the chair. "Enough of the melancholy air. There is a new life ahead! Those who live must continue on. You will, I hope, consent to be best man at the wedding?"

"I was hoping to give away the housekeeper," jibed Holmes. "Surely Thurston should be best man."

"Capital idea. Now I must be going. I have a consultation with a specialist in Harley Street in the morning."

"Not you, old man?"

"No, no, a patient of mine. But now I will bid you goodnight. That is, of course, unless I'm needed to burgle a mansion or capture a miscreant? No? Ah well, perhaps next time."

Holmes sat up late that night. Only two pipes would be attributed to this problem tonight. Watson had provided more information than he knew. Information that could be interpreted in at least two ways.

Holmes had agreed to Watson coming to visit again in a day or two, but tomorrow he would travel back to Sussex. Perhaps the bees would suggest something.

Chapter 16

Thurston

True to his word, Mercer did have information for Holmes that afternoon. Thurston, Watson's friend of many years - every Thursday billiard partner, English Billiard Champion and billiard table maker - was back in London. He would be happy to meet with Mr Holmes that evening at the bar of the Criterion Restaurant if Mr Holmes would then join him for dinner in the East Room. The Marble Hall with its fine mosaic ceiling was more to Holmes's liking, but this would do quite well.

At eight that evening, Holmes was in the very bar in which Watson had first heard from Stamford that there was a gentleman by the name of Sherlock Holmes who was looking to share rooms. That had been some 27 years ago.

Thurston was one who never seemed to get older. He was always a jovial fellow, quick of wit and ready with a helping hand. Holmes could not help but wonder what dark secrets lay below the surface. *Or maybe,* Holmes thought, *I have seen so much of evil that I can not accept good in a nearly pure form.*

"There you are, Holmes!" Thurston was immaculate of dress, clean-shaven and smiling from ear to ear.

"Good to see you, Thurston," replied Holmes. "I'm glad you could spare me some time."

"Well, your man - Mercer, was it? Yes, he made it all sound so mysterious I couldn't help but say yes. You know, I don't believe I've seen you since I waved you and Watson off to South Africa."

"Yes, it has been quite a while. But allow me." Holmes called the waiter over to order drinks. Thurston was obviously a regular since he ordered "the usual" and Holmes a whiskey and soda. When the drinks had come, Thurston wanted to drive the conversation to what Holmes required of him.

"You know, I have frequently told Watson how envious I was - oh, yes, envious is the right word. All the cloak and dagger and high society scoundrels, trips through the opium dens of Limehouse and mad dogs on the moor, you and he have such an adventurous time, while I, well, what do I do? Shoot billiards! How boring."

"Yes, and you have quietly contributed thousands to charities, old soldiers homes, and poor houses. You sir, are a scoundrel, a secret philanthropist!"

"Holmes, Holmes, please, you'll ruin my reputation. Don't you know I am a mad gambler, a gadabout, and a gigolo?" Thurston flushed at the praise from Holmes.

"But what is this business that only I can help with? As I said, Mercer was emphatic that I should meet you."

"As one of Watson's oldest friends, I know I may trust you," started Holmes. He went on to explain the allegations made by Campbell and his efforts to investigate. He explained the need for secrecy in the affair. Both the reputations of Watson and Mrs Hudson were at stake.

"Holmes," declared Thurston after listening to the story, "surely you of all people do not believe any of this. It is not even worthy of investigation."

"It is because it is so absurd that we must investigate. You know as well as I that the mere allegation in the papers brings discredit and scandal. We must put paid to this and before the allegation can be made public. Or," Holmes paused, "we must bring a killer to justice."

Thurston was dumb struck. "Why Holmes, I think you've gone mad!"

"You do not understand me, Thurston. I did not say I believe the allegation. But it will not do just to deny it. We must show there has been a fair and impartial review and the Doctor is exonerated or guilty."

"Yes, yes, I see what you mean. But what can I do?" Thurston leaned toward Holmes, gazing into his face.

"You were at the scene of the death of his first wife, Lucy, were you not?"

"Now, that was a tragedy. What a beautiful young woman! She was vibrant and exciting. Watson was a lucky man there. A little intimidating perhaps, Lucy was." Thurston stopped to drink and smile. "She could shoot, she could ride, and she loved the countryside. Not much on society, shall we say. One thought she felt more at home down at the stables than in 'the big house' as the Americans put it."

"Yes, I see, but can you tell me what happened? How did the accident occur?"

"Ah, pretty straight forward as far as that. John and Lucy always rode hard, liked to be to the front. Oh, never got out of their place, if you understand, but enjoyed the game.

"Now one of the things they liked to do was jump together whenever the obstacle allowed. Didn't matter what it was - fence, gate, fallen tree. It was kind of a thing with them. Most people don't like it. Distracting, you know, and dangerous, to be honest. Anyway, we were coming up on a gate and four or five had already gone over it. It was quite wide and the two of them should have been able to go over together easily, but for some reason John was a bit in front of Mary, which happens, hard to keep two unmatched horses together. Anyway, John was over first, Mary's horse's head was about at John's knee when suddenly the mare starts crow-hopping madly, crashes through the gate and down into the ditch. Couldn't have been a worse spot because just to the right of the gate that ditch was a good 20 feet to the bottom. All quite horrible." Thurston signalled for another of "the usual". "I was only two, maybe three, lengths behind. Saw it all and went as fast as I could for help and a gun. Very sad, very sad."

"Was this a place you had hunted before?"

"Oh, yes. Colonel Ross' place in Dartmoor. John and I were both members of the hunt."

"I understand that the horse had to be destroyed also."

"Broken leg. I was going to do it but Watson took the gun from me and unloaded half the revolver in the poor beast. Never seen Watson like that before or since. Quite a rage he was in. Grief I suppose."

"One last question, if you please Thurston, then we shall dine in peace. Did Watson seem short of funds?"

Thurston surveyed Holmes. It was obvious that he was considering how to answer.

"No more than usual. Let me put it this way. Watson is tight with a penny unless it is in the name of a good charity and then I have known him to be exceedingly generous. He does not, however, spend freely or bet largely that I have ever seen. So for all I know he could have a million pounds sterling in the bank or two shillings ha'penny."

"I understand completely. And now it is time for beef and roasted potatoes, I think."

Chapter 17

Lady Frances

The morning found Holmes on the train back to Sussex. He believed he knew what was to be known about Mary and Lucy. The most difficult inquiries were yet to come, Lady Frances and Malalai. Before he had started looking into the entire affair, Holmes would have said there was nothing to an allegation of an Indian wife, or was she Afghan? But now, with so much revealed, was it possible? That would have to wait for brother Mycroft.

As to Lady Frances, that certainly had been a singular affair. He was the one who had involved Watson in the bizarre ordeal. Lady Frances Carfax had been the last survivor of an old and distinguished family, that of the Earl of Rufton. She was a few years younger than he and Watson, had an adequate but modest income and a collection of Spanish jewellery of silver and diamonds. The Lady Frances travelled where she wished and seemed to have no burning interest nor favoured suitor. It was the old governess of Lady Frances, a Miss Dabney, who went to Holmes when her old charge suddenly stopped writing.

Holmes had requested Watson to travel to Lausanne, to the Hotel National. Watson would then travel to Montpelier and to Baden seeking clues as to the whereabouts of the Lady.

It eventually was discovered that an old acquaintance and would-be lover of Lady Frances, one Phillip Green, had unwittingly caused Lady Frances to go to Baden. He was an old suitor whom she wished to avoid. In Baden she fell in with two unscrupulous scoundrels posing as missionaries. Dr and Mrs Shlessinger were purported to be missionaries from South America. The "doctor" was wheelchair-bound and the act completely took in Lady Frances.

The Shlessingers turned out to be a confidence trickster from Australia named Holy Peters and a woman named Fraser. Lady Frances had willingly accompanied the pair to London, if for no other reason than to avoid her unwanted suitor. Here the infamous couple held Lady Frances captive while they began to sell off her jewellery.

It was Phillip Green, now aiding Holmes and Watson, who discovered both the location of the criminals and of the delivery of a coffin to the address. Together Holmes and Watson forced their way into the criminals' house. Lady Frances was their goal, for there could be no other alternative for the Shlessingers but the murder of their captive. But the doctor and the detective were unsuccessful. In the coffin that had been delivered was the body of an old woman - a former servant of Fraser's, or so they were told.

Holmes had spent the night in thought. *What had he missed?* There was a clue that had escaped him, but what? Then it came to him. Calling Watson to rush back to the house with him, the pair was just able to stop the funeral. Pulling the lid off the coffin they found not one, but two bodies inside. The clue had been the exceeding depth of the coffin, far too deep for only one frail creature. Lady Frances had been chloroformed and was only barely saved from being buried alive.

After a half hour's effort by Watson and having assured the safety of the lady, Holmes and Watson had turned her care over to Phillip Green. But when she was somewhat recovered she continued to insist that she wanted nothing to do with the man. She did, however, want to meet the good doctor who had saved her life. Watson was not displeased.

Once again, sighed Holmes, *a woman of beauty, moderate means and a treasure. How the scenario kept repeating.*

Before getting into Mr O'Brien's dog cart, he sent a wire. Hopefully Mercer would finally have made inroads as to the finances of one Dr John Hamish Watson.

Chapter 18

Money

Mercer thanked O'Brien and asked if he would wait. He expected his discussion with Holmes would not take long and that he would need to return to the station. O'Brien agreed but "would you think Mrs Hudson would give some tea to a poor working man?"

Mercer smiled to himself. The Irishman was nothing, if not persistent. "I'm sure, Mr O'Brien, that she will always have tea for you."

"Mr O'Brien," sounded the soft brogue, "don't you be bothering Mr Holmes' guests. You know I have tea in the back. Tie Dorothy to the rail and I'll bring a cup. Good morning to you, Mr Mercer."

"And to you, Mrs Hudson. Is Mr Holmes...?"

"In the bee shed taking some kind of count. I'll just go down and get him."

"No need, Mrs Hudson. I'll go round and talk to him." *Better to be away from her ears anyway*, thought Mercer.

Holmes was indeed in the workshop where he stored his supplies. He was seated at a table inspecting jars of honey and making notes in a ledger book.

"Come in, Mercer. I see you have some results for me."

The detective stepped into the shop and placed a pasteboard folder on the old wooden table cluttered with bottles.

Holmes glanced at the folder and returned his gaze to the honey jars.

"What is the short version?"

"Well, sir." Mercer reclaimed the folder and, opening it, sat down at the table. "Short version is that the doctor is well off. At least he is right now."

Holmes raised a single eyebrow.

"Meaning?"

"It's like this: It's been boom or bust for the Doctor." Mercer went into the folder. "Now, back when you first knew him, he was a bit down, not practicing medicine and all, and just having a half-pay pension.

128

Then he comes into some money and leaves for America. He is gone for a couple of years working in California."

"Yes, I loaned him the money to go to the aid of his brother, no mystery there, and he paid back the loan. Continue."

"Well, sir, he gets married when he gets back and has enough money to buy a small practice. But he makes a sizeable deposit in Cox and Company Bank." Mercer glanced up from his notes. "We've been lucky he's banked the same place all these years. I didn't need to spread your money quite as thin as otherwise. Anyway, during that time he's making a modest income from the practice but he is also spending money on 'investments', shall we say? He buys a piece of a number of horses, spends money at the tracks, and gets up with the folks who have much more than he has. Don't get me wrong, sir. He doesn't spend more than he takes in but the money was tight at times. Now when Mrs Watson - that is the first one - dies, there is a large deposit. Insurance, I suppose. I haven't been able to come up with a company name yet but I'm working on it."

"Does the same thing occur each time?" interrupted Holmes.

"Yes, sir. The policies aren't big, from what I can tell. Only a few thousand pounds. Not enough to make anyone think the poor women were killed for the money."

"A few thousand can be a lot of money to the right person, but go on."

"Well, sir, it really goes the same way each time. Now between his first and second and third wives, he had added writing to his income. The *Strand Magazine, Collier's* and some others were paying him very well for his stories about you. So he had that, the pension, and a small practice. The money from the writing was sent straight to his bank and I've copies of the deposits here."

Mercer tried to hand Holmes the papers, but they were just waved away.

"The money was sizeable, but it went out almost as fast as it came in. He made some very large transfers over the years that appear to be for horses. I base that on who the draughts were written to. There are also almost monthly draughts to stables for what was surely upkeep."

"Were there any over-draughts from the bank?"

"No, sir."

"Was he ever without funds?"

"No, sir."

"So each marriage brought additional wealth, each death brought a small amount of funds."

"True, sir."

"And while he spent almost all that came in, he was never in need. Does that sum it up?"

Mercer closed the folder and slouched back in his chair.

"Which brings us nowhere." Holmes inspected another jar. "Were most of Watson's transaction in cash then?"

"I'm afraid he would take out sizeable sums, so there is no paper trail as to where it went."

"Well, we do know he was good to his servants, but only paid them a moderate salary." Putting his last jar back in a box Holmes drew out his pipe.

"There are a few more things we must look at." He charged his pipe before continuing. "I want you to find out how many race horses he has owned. That will be simple, as the animals and owners are registered. Now if it is a company or syndicate that owns the animal, it will be more difficult, I admit. Second, I want you to put a man tracking the accident in Belgium that led to Lady Frances' death. I will give you a letter of introduction to an inspector in the Belgian police who may prove helpful."

While Holmes wrote a note at the table, Mercer took out his notebook and busily recorded the details that Holmes knew of the accident.

"Anything else, sir?"

"Did you ever talk to Watson's agent, Doyle?"

"No, sir. I decided not to talk to him as he is such good friends with the Doctor. I talked to a couple of the clerks and an editor by the name of Andrews. What they told me was that the Doctor frequently just made his deadlines and more than a couple of times missed them all together - causing them to have to rush to make their publication deadlines."

Holmes drew on the pipe as Mercer sat expectantly. It was Holmes who finally broke the silence.

"You have given me much to think about, but no answers."

"Sorry, Mr Holmes, but …"

"No, no, sir. You have done very well indeed. Much better than Watson ever could," he chuckled.

"Now you had best be off as the good doctor is to be here by the afternoon train and should he see you, he will be all curiosity."

Mercer left Holmes smoking at the table and, much to Mrs Hudson's relief, deprived her of the company of Mr O'Brien.

It was early afternoon when Watson appeared with his Gladstone bag for an overnight stay. This time Mr O'Brien did not stay and ask for tea.

Dinner that night was a fine affair of mutton. Holmes insisted that all three should eat together. They were the closest thing to family that he knew, except for Mycroft, and who could deny the betrothed of each other's company? As dinner ended, Martha insisted that Holmes and Watson retire to the porch with their cigars. The gentlemen complied, of course.

Hardly a word passed between the old friends as they watched the shades of night start to descend.

"You, Watson, still have that wonderful gift of silence. It is one of the greatest gifts that a man can possess."

"Thank you, Holmes, I think."

The two continued in silence until Martha joined them.

"Well, that's all done and we're ready for the morning."

"Would you two care to take a walk?" asked Holmes.

"I do believe we are being evicted, Mrs Hudson," smirked Watson.

"I am quite content where I am, Watson, and I know you wish to discuss things. Ferdinand and I claim the porch."

"Well, it was what I was going to suggest, Mr Holmes," piped up Martha. "John, will you escort me to the cliffs?"

The couple went arm in arm through the light of the three-quarter moon to the cliffs where they could be alone and themselves.

Watson could not believe his good fortune. He stood at the top of the cliffs watching a beautiful woman take in the moonlight. She finally turned to him and taking her in his arms, he held her close and kissed her. She returned the kiss, not with a peck, but with passion. He knew this was a woman who wanted that fiery love, that love where your body ached and you threw yourself into it heart and soul. The kiss went on as if it would never end, but when it did, there was instantly the desire for more.

Sitting upon a large rock the couple lost themselves in each other's arms.

"John, you are the man I have wanted for so long. All those years, when you married another, it hurt so."

"None of that matters, Martha. We are together now."

She tried to nestle deeper in his arms.

"Oh, I've brought you something. Just a little token."

"I don't need anything, John. I have you."

"Yes, I know," he said with a smile, "but it isn't right that I haven't given you a token of how I feel. It's just something I picked up in Afghanistan years ago."

Watson took a washed leather pouch out of his pocket and, opening it, took out a gold chain. On the chain was affixed a gold disk about two inches in diameter and in the centre of that was a ruby of roughly two carats. Around the ruby was an inscription in a language Martha had never seen, از خطرنـــاکتر عشـق است نفــرت.

"How beautiful, John! But I couldn't take something so expensive."

"Of course you can. I love you and want you to have it. Surely you won't disappoint me."

He placed the chain over her neck and she let him. Taking the disk in her hands she looked at it again.

"What does it say, John? Do you know?"

"Honestly, no. I do not. What I do know is that it is worn by the most beautiful woman in the world."

"Dr John Watson, I already said I'd marry you. You can cut the malarkey!" She smiled and kissed him again, another long lingering kiss.

"Ah, excuse me, but I must go to London tonight." It was Holmes standing behind them. The two sprang from their seats like school children caught playing instead of studying.

"You need a cow bell, Holmes."

"Sorry, Doctor. But Mycroft has need of me and I can just make the last train."

"But, Holmes," Watson looked at Martha, "I cannot stay here alone with the woman to whom I am engaged. What would people say?"

"What would Mr O'Brien say?" teased Holmes.

"Mr Holmes, you just go along and get your bag. The Doctor will be catching the same train. Now off with you."

"Watson, I believe you now have seen the woman's true colours. Bossy and possessive! It's not too late to back out."

"Never," replied Watson. "We will be along in a moment."

True to his word Watson and Martha were behind Holmes only by the time it took to kiss again.

A fifteen-minute walk brought the companions to the station.

"I'm sorry your visit was cut so short, Watson. Perhaps you can come back next week."

"I will try, certainly."

"Indian or Afghan?"

"What?"

"The necklace."

"Oh, Afghan, I think. At least that is where I got it. No idea what it says. Is there some adventure I can help you with?"

"Not that I know of. Mycroft had been gathering data for me and he must have something of significance or he would not have sent for me. A trivial affair."

"As trivial as the Naval Treaty?"

"Watson, hadn't I complimented you on your gift of silence?"

Chapter 19

Brother Mycroft

The coffee at the Diogenes Club the next morning was excellent, not that Holmes noticed. He had been up and about for hours, as was his habit in Sussex. Mycroft, however, would not be available before nine unless there was a national emergency - and there was not.

When the coffee had been poured in the Strangers Room, Sherlock allowed the waiter to retire. Once the doors were shut he turned a questioning gaze to his brother.

"The pastries are quite good this morning, Sherlock. Do try some."

"You have heard from your sources about Watson. I should much prefer to hear about that first."

"Yes, of course you would. Action, movement, jousting; how I envy you, brother! Even now you always want to jump into the fray. Well, I, sir, will have my treat whether you wish one or not."

"You've put on a few pounds since last year, you know. What, ten?"

"Eleven."

"Ah, and yet you still have time to help your poor brother. How kind."

"Oh, all right Sherlock, if you must jump straight into things."

Mycroft got up from the table and, with coffee cup in hand, repositioned his bulk by the window sill.

"I've been able to find three of the men who would be the most likely to know anything about this Afghan woman, Malalai. By the way, she was indeed Afghan, not Indian as Campbell claims. At any rate, as I have said, we found his old orderly Liam Murray in a western part of the States. His close friend Arthur is in Bermuda, and his former commander, Colonel Rowland, in India." Mycroft poured himself more coffee. "I shall start with the easy one first. Arthur McMullen was a lieutenant when he and Watson served together. McMullen was Indian Cavalry. At the time of Watson's departure, the lieutenant was 600 miles away and claims no knowledge of how the relationship between Watson and the girl ended. He believed the girl was married to an Indian Army Sergeant."

"And have you been able to confirm that?"

"Brother dear, you cut me to the quick." Mycroft pulled a paper from a file folder on the table. "A confirmation from our man in Peshawar. She was indeed married to a Sergeant of the 27th Punjab Infantry at Dakka. Colonel McMullen also admits he was in on Watson's little treasure hunt but says Watson..."

"Yes, I'm quite familiar with all that. Watson keeps a small box with two rubies in it as a memento. So the Colonel knows nothing except that there was a relationship at one time."

"Correct." Mycroft returned the paper to the folder.

"And Colonel Rowland?"

"Ah, a little more information there but not likely what you are looking for. Colonel Rowland was Watson's regimental commander at the time the Doctor saved the girl from a certain death. He does believe that Watson was, shall we say, 'sweet', on the girl. But had no reason to believe the relationship had any substance and there was certainly no inappropriate behaviour on Watson's part."

"So there is nothing there either."

"Wait, dear brother, wait." Mycroft got a sly grin as he sat back at the table. "The girl disappeared on the very day that Watson left Dakka with his treasure box. Oh, Rowland doesn't know anything about the treasure to this day. Only a handful of people do. Rowland remembers the disappearance because the woman had been working in the native clinic operated by army medical staff. When she vanished the 'inside joke', if you will, was that she followed Watson."

Holmes sat quietly, taking all this in. "You know, Mycroft, that Watson had given her and her new husband a share of the jewels. It could be just as likely that she took those jewels and ran away or that her new husband, in possession of what to him was a vast sum, did away with her."

"Of course, Sherlock, but unfortunately neither you, nor I, are in Afghanistan to follow a twenty-eight year old trail."

Holmes sighed. "And Murray? Is he able to shed any light on this?"

"As to Murray, as you know, he delivered Watson to the steamship in Bombay which returned him to England. He then returned to his regiment and eventually retired. He claims that he was as mystified by the disappearance of the girl as anyone." Mycroft picked up a letter. "He does add that Sergeant Guhkta appeared to be truly distraught. Even took a leave to search for the girl. He says that the Sergeant never gave any indication of having the jewels that Watson gave him. No kind of outlandish spending or anything."

"Yes, quite interesting. Most criminals do not have the intelligence to hold onto newly gained wealth. Instead they give themselves away by spending."

"Now, Sherlock, since I have only been able to piece together information of this treasure found by Watson, perhaps you would enlighten me. If he found a treasure while in the service he would be entitled to ten percent, but the treasure itself would belong to the Crown."

"No, no, Mycroft, the story of the treasure is Watson's to tell. And it went to very good use, not to Watson's." It was Sherlock's turn to pour himself more coffee.

"After all," he continued, "would Watson have needed to seek a partner to share rooms if he were a wealthy man? I think not."

"Perhaps the Doctor is a shrewder man than we have ever given him credit for."

"Perhaps, but let me see if I may summarize." Sherlock ticked the points off on his fingers. "There was a girl, she and Watson were not married, and in fact she married another."

Mycroft nodded, Holmes continued.

"The girl had no money of her own but what was given to her by Watson. The girl disappeared the day Watson left and there are at least three possibilities as to why or how."

"Four, if one includes a random act of violence."

"Agreed. In short, we have no proof of anything."

The two brothers sat for some moments as if a pair of bookends, each leaning back in his chair, arms on the rails, fingertips touching and eyes closed. It was Mycroft who finally broke the silence.

"Your next move is Anstruther, of course."

"Yes, he helped with Lady Frances' recovery. I shall talk to him next."

Chapter 20

Anstruther

Paddington Station is the terminus of the Great Western Railway. Near it is the former home of Robert Louis Stevenson. Nearby is the Edgware Road Station of the Metropolitan Railway. Here, too, by Warwick Crescent, was the home of Robert Browning before his marriage. Aside from these facts, *Baedeker's* states: "The winding Harrow Road traversed by a tramway to Wembley, Sudbury and Harrow leads through the busy but uninteresting district of Paddington." Possibly *Baedeker's* found it uninteresting to the tourist trade because of the fact that is was mostly residential. What better place for a family doctor's surgery? People like to have their doctors close at hand.

145

Here is where Holmes travelled to find Dr Anstruther. The doctor had frequently acted on behalf of Watson in those times when Holmes had sent for his companion. Watson had reciprocated on the few times that his neighbour required his help, the occasional holiday and such.

Anstruther, like Watson, and if Holmes were to admit it, like himself, was not retired. A doctor seems to have a most difficult time leaving the profession. Holmes had wired and received a reply that, yes indeed, the doctor could make himself available after his morning rounds and hoped that one o'clock would be satisfactory.

Holmes, in turn, hoped that Anstruther's sense of propriety would keep him from talking to Watson, even though they were old friends. Once again, the story of a book would be seen through quickly.

Promptly at one in the afternoon, Holmes was admitted to the surgery and shown straight back to the doctor's office.

"Good of you to see me, Doctor. I do hope it is not too inconvenient."

Anstruther came out from behind his desk and the two shook hands. Anstruther could not have looked more like Watson had they been brothers. His hair was still dark, military moustache, a few pounds overweight, but obviously a man who enjoyed exercise and sport. Having completed the niceties and Holmes being offered and turning down some tea, or something stronger, the men sat at the small consulting table.

"I do hope this is not a professional visit, Mr Holmes. You certainly give the appearance of well-being and a healthy life style."

"As to that, Doctor, it is unfortunately a professional visit in a sense." Anstruther seemed taken aback. "But for me, doctor, not for you."

"For you?" Anstruther seemed confused. "Has someone brought a case against me? I can't imagine..."

"Not against you, sir, but against our mutual friend Watson."

"Balderdash! Watson is a fine surgeon. Not the best perhaps, but..."

"If I may continue, Doctor Anstruther." Holmes did, explaining in as much detail as he felt prudent what the allegation was against their friend. Those things he had already discovered about his friend he withheld in order not to influence the doctor's responses.

"And this man would ruin the happiness of two people because it might interfere with a potential gain to himself? That is what you are saying, is it not?"

"Perhaps, but let us say he is concerned for his aunt."

"Balderdash, I say it again. What can I do for you, Mr Holmes?"

"You were familiar with two of Watson's wives - Mary, when she and he lived next door and I understand you consulted with Watson in the treatment of Lady Carfax."

"True on both counts."

"Let us begin with Mary. Was there any disharmony between her and Watson? Any discord that you could tell?"

"Quite the contrary, Mr Holmes. I have never seen a more loving couple. She was so quiet and sweet. The servants loved her, as did my wife. Mary never seemed to mind anything Watson did, whether it was to run off to a racing meet or share one of your adventures."

Anstruther was searching Holmes' face. "She was not well, you know," he continued. "Heart troubles. Ah, but she loved her garden too. All hours of the day or evening you could see her working out there or sitting in the little gazebo Watson had built. He'd sit out there with her many an evening. No, Mr Holmes," Anstruther shook his head violently as he sat back. "Impossible to conceive of Watson doing such a horrid thing. I wouldn't believe it if he told me himself."

"I understand and am much of the same disposition. However, I have another question. Did you ever know Watson to be short of funds?"

Anstruther thought for a moment before he responded. A smile came on his face. "Watson did borrow £10 from me on one occasion. He was running to catch a train with you from Paddington Station. He asked me to look after his rounds and since he had no time to get to a bank, he asked me for the loan. I think he wrote about it as *The Boscombe Valley Mystery* or some such."

"Now, that does sound like Watson. As to the Lady Frances, did she ever make a full recovery from her ordeal?"

"Ah," Anstruther signed deeply, "there I am afraid the answer is no. But how can one wonder at that? To be confined in a coffin with a dead woman and almost buried alive yourself. The terror of it! It's a wonder she wasn't truly mad afterward. Then, too, there was the lack of oxygen. Without proper oxygen flow to the brain great damage is done. Many times irreparable damage."

"And Watson consulted you for what reason? No offense doctor, but you are not a specialist of the mind."

"No, Mr Holmes, I am certainly not. But Watson consulted me more to keep his own sanity than to keep hers." Anstruther was becoming nervous and rose from his chair to pace the room. "When normal medical techniques failed us, he ventured into the realm of the alienist, a Harley Street man. I'm afraid the complexities of psychology is not my area of expertise. It seemed to help some but she continued to have frequent nightmares. She quite clung to John at the time. She saw him as her saviour. She idolized the poor man."

"And how did that sit with Watson?"

"That's why he would come to see me. He loved her deeply, but found her at times suffocating. Well, you know, he loved to just take off and go to the Continent and catch the racing season or go adventuring with you." Anstruther grinned at Holmes.

"I'm afraid during that particular period of Watson's life I did not keep up with him well. Did he own many horses?"

"Oh, yes." Anstruther opened a cabinet and pouring himself a whiskey offered one to Holmes who nodded.

"Let me see now," the doctor murmured. "I don't believe he had more than two or three at any one time but over the years he must have had, oh, twelve or fifteen. Usually just a piece of each, but he wholly owned one that was an offspring of that Silver Blaze horse. Sorry, can't remember the name."

The doctor handed over the whiskey glass and sat back down.

"You say he went to races on the continent?"

"Yes, um, Belgium, Holland, France. I think. He was supposed to go to Italy one time but that fell through."

"And Lady Frances?"

"She always went. Sad, that's where she contracted tetanus - in Belgium I mean."

"Do you know what happened? I only know there was a carriage accident of some sort."

"Well, I only have the story second-hand of course. Seems that Watson's horse was to run and on the way to the course… - let me think. Yes, West Flanders, isn't it?" The doctor got up and pulled a large atlas from a bookshelf. "Yes, Ostend, that's where it was. They have a large race course there. Anyway," he placed the book back. "Watson and Frances had taken a carriage out to the track but just before they got there, the carriage was struck by a tram. Don't ask me how. Watson was fine, but Lady Frances received some cuts on her arm that required stitches. The short of it is she became hysterical and had to be sedated. Watson missed the race, his horse lost, and Lady Frances contracted tetanus. She died in Lausanne the next week."

"I thought it was common practice for the last ten years to give a tetanus shot when someone received stitches?"

"Oh, it is, Mr Holmes, but Watson said she wouldn't let them come near her with a needle. All he could do was to get her to let them stitch her up."

"I see."

"Too bad really about the whole trip."

"How's that?"

"Watson was supposed to have gone by himself. I recommended it to him. 'Leave her this time,' I said. He was in desperate need of a break. The constantly needing to take care of her was telling on him. Had things gone on as they were, I'm not sure we wouldn't have had to provide care for him."

"And the tetanus showed up later?"

"Yes, it usually appears in about seven days. That's what happened in this case." The doctor nodded slowly. "Why the toxoid did not work I cannot say. You know, these foreign countries don't do as well with their medications as our British firms."

Holmes thanked the doctor for his hospitality and was leaving when Anstruther called from the door to his office. "Oh, and he paid back the tenner!"

Holmes smiled, waved, and made his way to the train station. He was hoping Mercer would have word tonight from Belgium.

Chapter 21

The Belgian Connection

Once again Lestrade was waiting for Holmes at the Langham Hotel upon his return. Holmes saw the Scotland Yard detective sitting in the lobby. His bowler in his lap, he gave every appearance of sleeping. Holmes walked quietly to the side of the large upholstered chair and said nothing.

"It's a technique, Mr Holmes." Lestrade grinned and looked up. "You've probably used it yourself. Keeps people from nattering at you."

"Well, join me in the smoking room and I shall refresh you instead."

Lestrade got out of the soft chair as if his bones ached and followed into the next room. Holmes, much to Lestrade's disappointment, ordered two coffees and sat near the empty fireplace.

"How did it go with Sir Melville? Not well, I venture."

"No, Mr Holmes. Seems our Mr Campbell is somewhat influential in the banking district. He's not exactly a big-wig, but well known enough to cause problems."

Holmes nodded his understanding. Lestrade was putting everything on the line to help Watson. *One way or another*, Holmes thought, *he must succeed.*

"Did you get the official report of the accident in Belgium?"

"Yes, Mr Holmes. In frog, it was, so I had to get it translated." Lestrade extracted two large sheets of paper from his inside coat pocket. "Nothing really to report, though. Seems the doctor rented the carriage for the day himself. He was the one driving. It was a," he looked at the paper, "one horse brougham. Nothing he shouldn't have been able to handle." He looked at the paper again. "Seems there was an argument afterwards as to who had the right of way, but the electric tram clipped the carriage and over it went. Horse was okay."

"I'm delighted to hear that!"

"Anyway," continued an obviously flustered Lestrade, "it wasn't of any consequence. Lady Frances was taken to hospital and received some stitches. That was it."

Holmes took out his cigarette case. "Perhaps Mercer will have more information. He should be back sometime tonight. I sent him to the scene. Ostend has a good ferry service with us. But in the meantime, Chief Inspector, will you join me for dinner?"

"I'd be delighted, Mr Holmes."

"But perhaps your wife is expecting you home."

"If there is one thing she has learned in 40 years... it's don't expect me home!" Lestrade thought himself a wit.

It was during a fine crepes dessert in the hotel dining room that the two were interrupted by the arrival of the private detective.

"May I join you, gentlemen?" he inquired.

"Only if you will have a cognac and one of these fine cigars," replied the host.

The three waited quietly until the waiter had served the drinks before they conferred.

"What were your results?" Holmes was blunt and to the point.

Mercer removed his ever present notebook and flipped a few pages. He canted his head and gave Holmes an inquisitive look.

"Queer duck you sent me to, Mr Holmes. Don't get me wrong, his English is okay but he fair wore me out with his bit about 'little grey cells'."

"Yes, I'm sure he would. But he is one of the most logical and orderly thinkers I have ever met." Holmes turned to Lestrade. "He should be near retirement also. But continue. Was he of any help?"

"As to that, yes. Seems he was on duty that day. It was a special race they have on the national day. It was called... here it is... the Grand International d'Ostende. Dr Watson had a horse running that day, one 'Soothsayer', placed sixth and out of the money. Now this friend of yours says the accident was completely the doctor's fault, but being a foreigner and having some notoriety as an author, they decided to just call things done and blame nobody." He looked to Lestrade. "We know how that works, eh?"

Lestrade nodded.

"Now there were two things the Inspector thought strange. First was the accident itself. The entrance to the track was to the left of where it all happened, but the Doctor crossed the tram tracks to the right. Said the horse just wouldn't respond. 'Course that does happen, they are strange creatures. Second, when they went to the hospital Dr Watson insisted on doing the stitching on his wife."

"Nothing so odd about that," piped up Lestrade. "He's a doctor, you know. It's his wife. He wants to be sure it's done right and no mistake. I'd have done the same if I were a doctor."

"Perhaps," breathed Holmes. "Did he know anything about Switzerland?"

"Not really, sir. Just that there was a report from a Dr," he looked at his notes again, "Van Dyke. He informed the Belgian police that the lady died of tetanus as a result of the accident. Thought they should have it for their report."

"Wasn't in what they gave me!" interjected Lestrade.

"Well, that was what the man said."

All three men sat for a few moments with their own thoughts. Holmes was the first to rise.

"Gentlemen, I leave in the morning for Belgium and Switzerland. Mercer, if you'll come along to my room, I have a few additional tasks for you."

"And for me, Mr Holmes?" It was almost a plea from Lestrade.

Holmes looked at his watch. "For you Lestrade, you can inform Sir Melville that this case will be ended in 96 hours. Now, if you will excuse us."

Chapter 22

The Continent

The trip to Dover, then by ferry, to the Belgian port of Ostend was uneventful. The port had been fought over continuously through the centuries due to its deep water and critical location. As early as 1836, the railroad to Brussels made it the main port in Belgium. Holmes would eventually catch the train to Brussels, but first he would meet his friend at the Hippodrome Wellington, the horse racing venue where Watson and Lady Frances had met with tragedy.

As in London, a single whistle blast brought up a taxi cab and Holmes gave instruction to the driver. It was the time for holidays and the town was filled with people from the Belgian and Dutch inlands seeking the beaches. Still, it took only a few minutes to reach the castle-like entrance to the race course. Built in 1883, the venue had all the appearance of a walled city whose main gate required the passage through a portcullis. From the left tower of the gate flew the Belgian flag. A bridge took visitors from the main street up to the entrance, giving the impression of crossing a moat. Down the centre of the street were the tracks and overhead the wires of the electric tram.

As he alighted from the taxi, Holmes was greeted by a tiny figure in the dress uniform of a Chief Inspector. He was an exquisite figure to behold: dark blue uniform, gold braid, polished belt and kepi. His shoes sparkled in the sunlight.

"Mon ami! Mon ami! How good it is to see you, my friend!" The little inspector was no more than five feet four inches with a lightly waxed military moustache and pomaded hair. "When I received your wire I told my superior I must go to Ostend and be there when my great friend arrives!"

The inspector had removed his white gloves and was violently shaking Holmes by the hand.

"Good to see you, Inspector, but as I said in the cable, I merely wanted to visit the scene of the accident so I might better understand what occurred. I have always believed seeing something in person is most helpful. The descriptions of others may prove faulty."

"Ah, it is true, that. Yes, in such a situation as this, I agree. Most crimes however, they require thought and the psychology."

"I could not agree more. If you remember, we both came to the same conclusion about the Countess Roeske's diamonds. Yet I was in London and you in Brussels."

"Yes, my friend, but we may talk of old times on the train. For now, what may I show to you?"

"I believe I have already seen it." Holmes turned toward the gates of the Hippodrome. "That to the right and below the walking gate, I take it, is for carriages." He pointing with his stick. "And Watson's brougham was approaching on this side from the tram tracks. He should easily have gone down the hill to the left, but the horse went right and crossed in front of the tram."

"Yes. But horses are so unpredictable. I have never liked to trust my well-being to animals."

"The carriage was hit in the front or the back?"

"The back, behind where sits the good doctor. He was very fortunate. As was the Mrs Watson. She was quite hysterical, even for a woman, mon ami. But I understand she was already ill."

"Why were you here?"

"Oh, merely because of the great race day. I had brought some extra police with me to help with the crowds. You know such events always have more than their share of pickpockets and how do you say, charlatans?"

"Of course. Well, my friend, shall we go to the train station? I must get on to Lausanne as soon as possible. I am afraid that the patience of Sir Melville is wearing a bit thin."

"Ah, he is one that does not appreciate the need to let the little grey cells function in their own good time."

"Definitely not!"

~ ~ ~ ~ ~ ~ ~ ~

From Brussels to Lausanne, Holmes had naught to do but review where he was on the case. He had almost all the pieces. He would not decide nor theorize until he had the final parts. Once again he wondered at the parts of Watson's life of which he had never been aware. He thought he knew Watson and took the rest for granted. He looked out the window into the night and wondered if he would find more surprises at Lake Geneva.

Dr Van Dyke was much younger than Holmes had expected, perhaps 32 or 33 years old. He had a pleasant disposition, a winning smile and the nurses of his surgery (there were two) both seemed infatuated with him. Holmes was sure the young man was the heartthrob of his female clients. While bright and cheerful with Holmes, he by no means tried to ingratiate himself, he knew the difference between male and female clients. Van Dyke would go far.

Having been shown to the doctor's inner office, Holmes was struck by its lack of personality. The walls were almost bare except for a few lithographs of mountain scenes.

"Yes, Mr Holmes. I do not display who I am in my office. I have found it is distracting to the patient and may be disconcerting also to me."

"Interesting, Doctor, but I did not come here to read your life story by the pictures on your wall or the cigarette ash in your tray."

"I'm relieved. Your friend, Dr Watson had made you seem almost super human."

"Other than the obvious facts that you are not Swiss but Austrian, went to school in England - Oxford I should say - are unmarried, and had Kaiser Schnitzel for lunch, I know little about you."

Van Dyke roared with laughter, looked down at his waistcoat and tried to remove the evidence of his diet.

"My accent, no ring, and," he pointed at himself, "a sloppy eater. Wonderful. But come, Mr Holmes, you've journeyed a long way. How may I help you?"

Holmes decided on a direct approach. "I understand you were working at the hospital here as an internist four years ago when Dr Watson brought in his wife for treatment of tetanus."

"That is correct, sir. Horrible case, horrible death. If one is not mad before one goes through the torture of tetanus, you are made so before you die."

"This was the case with Mrs Watson?"

Van Dyke hesitated. "Yes," he uttered slowly.

"Come, come, Doctor, I need to know what happened."

"Might I ask exactly why, Mr Holmes? Even after death I do not usually discuss a patient or their illness. Now, four years later, there are questions?"

"To be blunt, Doctor, I am working on behalf of Scotland Yard. Certain allegations have been made against Dr Watson and I have been charged with finding the truth."

"You astound me, sir. Could this be? Dr Watson was beside himself with worry and grief. He never left her for the three days until her death." Van Dyke shook his head.

"Be that as it may, Doctor, I must answer the questions, and to do that, I need your help. Will you help me?"

The doctor considered for a moment. "Ja, what do you need to know?"

"When Watson brought in Lady Frances, what were the symptoms?"

"Symptoms? Pah! She was already in distress. As I remember, there had been some kind of an accident a week before. Carriage, I think. Anyway, when they arrived at the hospital she was already suffering from muscle spasm in the jaw. I believe you call it lockjaw. We immediately treated her with tetanus toxoid. For some reason, Mr Holmes, she failed to respond. Most patients survive and will be able to function again in about four weeks. Mrs Watson though...." He shook his head again. "It was particularly virulent. We lost her in less than seventy-two hours. She went through it all, sir, tearing muscles, fractured bones, arching back, spasms, sweating, and fever. It was horrible to watch. And Dr Watson never left her side. He was there to the end.

"I'll tell you, Mr Holmes," he leaned back in his leather chair, "I've never seen such a case before or since."

"And when the lady arrived, were you the one who made the initial diagnosis?"

"No, sir. Dr Watson knew what it was right off, though any first-year medical student could have seen it for himself."

"And the lady was buried here?"

"Oh, no, cremated. I went to the service. Felt badly for the doctor. He really knew so few people here."

"Have you ever had another case where the toxoid did not work?"

"As a matter of fact, no, I have not. But some people just do not respond to certain medications. I wish we knew why."

"One last question, Doctor," Holmes was grave to the extreme.

Van Dyke turned to Holmes, an uncomfortable look on his face. "The answer to the question you are going to ask is yes..... strychnine."

"And was it tested for?"

"No."

Holmes thanked the doctor for his help and considered his next move. Looking at this watch, he decided on the train station. He would have one more consultation with Lestrade, Mercer and Mycroft. Then it would be time to confront Watson.

Chapter 23

Home

By late the following evening Holmes was once more ensconced in the Langham Hotel. He had requested that the desk clerk call Lestrade and have him come to the Diogenes Club at ten of the clock. Mercer would be waiting in the lobby of the hotel and Mycroft was expecting them in the Stranger's Room.

Holmes waved Mercer along as he exited the lift and strode quickly toward the front door, telling the doorman he wished a hansom cab. The man blew his whistle twice.

"Evening, Mr Holmes."

Holmes merely nodded to Mercer. He did not speak until they were in the cab.

"This will give us a few more moments and a little more privacy," stated Holmes. "Have you been able to find the other information?"

"That I have, sir, but it's no different than before, really. His current balance at Cox & Co is over £10,000. He had a deadline last week for a story what he missed by three or four days, but that seems usual for him. I also put a man outside his surgery like you asked and his practice seems good. In the last two days he's had almost two score patients." Mercer retrieved his notebook as the horse moved slowly through the traffic. "He has one woman what is a housecleaner and cook. She doesn't live in, comes early, and leaves supper on the kitchen table if he says he wants it." Mercer glanced quickly at Holmes, who sat impassively, then went on. "The doctor also has two girls what work for him in the surgery. One is a trained nurse, the other a bookkeeper and receptionist.

"And they are paid well?"

"Cacy, that's my man, Cacy says he couldn't get a number but the housekeeper says she is open to an offer from a 'handsome man like him'." Mercer could see Holmes didn't find the remark as humorous as he did. "Anyway, the pay is good."

"And the horses?"

"That's been more difficult that ought to be, sir. There are nine I can prove but some of these deals are hidden by corporations as you said. It will take more digging."

"Excellent," Holmes finally replied as the cab stopped in front of the Diogenes Club. "No need to go on with the search for horses. We know what we need to know. Please come along, and bring your notebook. We may have more to do, though I doubt it."

The pair was admitted to the club and Holmes, without waiting, headed for the inner sanctum where Lestrade and Mycroft waited.

"Ah, brother Sherlock, there you are." Mycroft was sitting behind the table that at times served as the map of the British Empire. Lestrade, glass in hand, rose from a red leather Queen Anne chair when the door opened.

"Brother, Lestrade. Please sit down, Lestrade. Mycroft, I believe a little stimulus all around would do us well."

"Certainly." Mycroft rang and then the four men sat in an uneasy silence until the door had once again closed behind the waiter.

Lestrade was the first to break the silence. "Well, Mr Holmes, have we done with it? Or has your trip proved something else?"

"Let us say, it has confirmed nothing one way or the other."

Lestrade slumped in his chair.

"Strychnine, of course," said Mycroft.

"Yes."

"What?" Lestrade came out of his chair.

"Sit down, good fellow." Mycroft waved his large hand. "Yes, but no way to confirm or deny, as you said with the body cremated."

"Now look here!"

"Lestrade, large doses of strychnine would cause many of the same symptoms as tetanus. The toxoid would have no effect and the patient would die." Mycroft sipped his drink again as Lestrade turned to Sherlock.

"Watson is a doctor, Lestrade." Holmes put his glass on the table. "A well-known doctor, not for his surgery, but for his writing, I admit. But well-known none the less. So," he stood to pace the floor, "a well-known doctor brings his wife to hospital. She has been injured, he says she has tetanus and stays though the treatment. He is obviously concerned. And when she dies, her ashes are spread on the lake she loved. None of this is suspicious and yet, from the point of view of an evil frame of mind, you have the murder plot of a cheap penny dreadful." Holmes stood looking out the window while the other three men were lost in thoughts of their own.

Mycroft looked at Lestrade, then at his brother's back at the window.

"Let me pursue this logically, one point at a time."

Holmes turned from the window and retook his chair. Mercer held the notebook and pencil and Lestrade moved his chair slightly forward.

Holmes deferred to his brother. "Go ahead."

"Yes, then. Was Watson materially better off with each death? Only slightly." He looked at the other three who all nodded their heads. "Is there any pattern to the deaths? No. One could say two involved horses, but they were very dissimilar. The carriage accident was very unlikely to cause a death. Was there another woman whom Watson was desirous of marrying? No, in fact there is considerable time between his marriages." Mycroft looked around the room once more. "Gentlemen, there is no basis to this accusation against a fine man. That is my opinion. Perhaps you each have a different one?"

Lestrade shifted in his chair. All eyes went to him. He cleared his throat.

"It's like this, I like cases that are clean cut. A bugger done it or he didn't, but here we have no proof either way. I know you shouldn't have to prove you did nothing, know what I mean? But it would be cleaner if we were able to. Campbell could still make an allegation and all we can say is 'no, don't think he did'."

"And you, Mercer?" Holmes looked to his assistant.

"Afraid I'm a lot like Lestrade here, sir. I'm convinced the Doctor done nothing at all. Wife, or should I say, wives, just died of different things. Bad luck is all. But I would like a piece of hard evidence to put up that Campbell's nose."

"And you, Sherlock?" Mycroft sat like a Buddha in his chair, fingers interlocked and an inscrutable smile.

"Does a man's character account for nothing? Yes, we all see the facts, they are plain. There is no proof of any crime and yet," he paused. "When one adds imagination, a skill I have often accused poor Lestrade here of lacking, it is all possible. That is until we remember who we are talking about. Do each of you really entertain the fact that the same Doctor we all know, who fought in Afghanistan and South Africa, who has stood by each of us in crisis, who took a bullet for me in our capture of Killer Evans could be guilty of such a series of crimes? No, gentlemen. A man's character does have meaning. Just as we know Campbell's true colours, we know Watson's."

"That we do, Mr Holmes. I'm with you there." Lestrade rested his glass on the table. "At least we have what we need to counter any charge made by this perfidious little windbag." Lestrade turned to Mercer. "I don't suppose I might press on your time a bit? I'd like to have your help when I write up my report for Sir Melville."

"Considering it's you, old man, I'll only charge double my usual fee," laughed Mercer.

The two men got up to leave, each shaking hands with Holmes.

"You've done a fine job, Sherlock," commented Mycroft once the other two had left.

"Perhaps, but I have one more job to do. I must face my friend and tell him all that has happened. I hope he will understand."

"Come, come, Sherlock. It is Watson. He will know you have done what is best."

"I wonder?"

Chapter 24

Dinner with Watson

Holmes had considered inviting Lestrade to dine with him and Watson the night following the meeting at the Diogenes Club but decided against it. Lestrade had risked everything by calling in Holmes but this discussion called for finesse, not a skill Lestrade had cultivated on the streets of London.

Holmes decided on Simpson's again. After all, it was Watson's favourite. As he waited for his friend to appear he could not help but wonder how Watson would take the news of the investigation. Surely he would be offended by Campbell's allegation, but would he also be put-off by Holmes not telling him about it? He was soon to find out.

"Holmes," greeted Watson from several feet away. "I was delighted to get your invitation. I'd no idea you were still in town." He took a seat as the wine steward approached.

"A burgundy, I think, Dominick. What do you say, Watson?"

"Anything's fine by me."

"Good old Watson. Alright, you pick it out, Dominick. I trust you completely."

The steward left as Watson continued his interrogation of Holmes. "So, what foul deed does Mycroft have you working on? Can I be of help?"

"Watson, I have a most delicate matter to lay before you. It is a task I have not taken lightly."

"You seem so serious, Holmes. Please, what can I do?"

"It is not you, Watson. It is I. I have been investigating you."

"Me? Whatever for? You're joking, surely." Watson's face was the very reflection of his perplexion.

"You know a man by the name of Colm Campbell, do you not?"

"I can't say that... oh, a cousin or nephew or some such of Martha's, is he not? But what could he..."

Holmes held up a restraining hand as the wine steward did his duty. As the man poured, Holmes continued.

"I have taken the liberty of already ordering," Holmes smiled. "For the last two decades, you have always referred to the menu and then always ordered the same thing."

Watson returned the smile until the man left.

"What is going on, Holmes?"

Sherlock took a deep breath and started the tale from the beginning. He left nothing out. Mercer, Lestrade standing up for him, (this at least brought a smile), Mycroft, and the investigation into each death: Malalai, Lucy, Mary, and Lady Frances. Watson seemed to become awed, then angry, then disbelieving. His shoulders sank under the weight as each woman was talked about. When Holmes had finished, there was nothing but silence for a long time.

Finally, Watson looked at his friend of so many adventures and years.

"Why, Holmes, could you not have come to me with all this? I feel so betrayed. I would have bared all, told all. Do you think I could have held back? Have I not always been true to our friendship?"

"I could not come to you, Watson. There was no evidence of any wrongdoing. I knew in my heart that there would not be. But had I told you, there are those who would have said I allowed you to manipulate the truth, to force the conclusion that you were innocent, and I would not have someone else try to interpret facts not in evidence, to use innuendo instead of truth. No, my friend, I did not do this with a light heart."

Holmes shifted slightly in his chair, and then went on. "I learned, though, that I had never paid proper attention to the one man I considered my only friend."

Watson looked up with a quizzical smile.

"The horses, eh? No, I never thought you would understand. Your interests, until the bees, had been so eclectic. You bored easily. How could you understand a single fascination that lasted a lifetime? And then, there was a bit of gambling with them.

"They did eat up the money, though, I will admit. Sometimes one does not stop to think properly. Feed, trainers, transport, it all adds up. Oh, I admit I had my share of bad horses. I have spent more than I have made on them. And too, there were bad investments. I didn't always concentrate on my practice, but you were partly to blame, you know. Oh, yes. Don't give me that look. 'Watson, come if convenient; if not convenient, come all the same,' or some such. It is hard for a patient to take seriously a doctor who is always gadding about or taking his time writing of mysteries. Yes, you were not faultless. But that is all long gone, Holmes!" Watson slapped his hand on the table. The patrons nearly were startled and looked askance.

"And now what do I do? Do I marry the woman? Will Campbell make trouble for me and her anyway? What does Lestrade's report say?

"As to that, he brought me a copy, which I have read," responded Holmes. "It clearly says there is no evidence against you and, for a policeman, it is well written. There can be no question as to your innocence."

The waiter appeared and placed plates in front of the two diners. Watson made no move.

"Do not let this stop you, Watson. It was a callous move by a little man. If you do not marry, you deprive yourself of the companionship of a wonderful woman, and you will break a great lady's heart. I beg you to not act in haste or anger of the moment."

"I must take time to think, Holmes. My emotions are playing havoc with my reason."

Watson picked up a fork and moved peas around on his plate for a moment. "You know, Holmes, I do know what that inscription is on the medallion I gave to Martha." He paused to look at his friend. "It is Farsi. It says, 'Love is more dangerous than hate'." He looked at his plate. "Somehow it didn't seem appropriate, but it is a lovely piece."

He continued without looking at Holmes. "I think I shall go now. I have much to think about. If you will excuse me."

He rose from the table. Holmes did not move and chose to say no more.

~ ~ ~ ~ ~ ~ ~ ~

The following week, as Holmes looked at the post Mrs Hudson had brought from the village he saw an envelope in Watson's hand addressed to him. The letter was short.

My Dear Holmes,

This is just a note to let you know that I have informed Mrs Hudson that our engagement, for my own reasons, must be called off. I know that I may rely on your discretion.

As Always,

Your Friend

John

From the room at the back of the house came a gentle sobbing.

"Watson, Watson, Watson," thought Holmes. *"Why?"*

Chapter 25

Deathbed

On the 5th of August, 1929, an old man of 75 years named Sherlock Holmes received the following letter which he found in a small, carved, wooden box delivered by post. Holmes placed the box on the table and laid out its contents before reading the letter.

King Edward VII

Memorial Hospital

Hamilton, Bermuda

My Dear Holmes,   24 July 1929

If you have received this, I have already passed. I have asked Arthur to place this letter in the small Afghan wedding box in which I kept the two rubies and the phial with the two bullets which I once showed you. He will have kept his promise, I know and you now have a small keepsake of me.

In the box you will also find the Afghan pendant I once gave to Martha, a twenty dollar gold piece from the San Francisco Mint, a pearl, and a Spanish silver ring.

You, of course, will immediately know what all these things represent. But, my friend, you only think you know. You see, Holmes, I did kill them. Each and every one. I was never quite sure if you were convinced of my innocence until you asked for my assistance in 1914 with the German spy ring. It was then I knew you still believed in me.

It was the money, old friend. It is as simple as that. The first one wasn't. Poor girl, she had married Guhkta. She should have been satisfied but the day our caravan left Dakka, she tried to follow us. It was an accident, I assure you. That first night out I caught her near my tent, we argued, she tried to make a scene. I only wanted to quiet her but when I grabbed for her, she fell and hit her head on a rock. I placed her body well off the road. When I did, I found the washed leather bag I had given her husband with a share of the treasure we had found. I kept it.

Perhaps it was the warfare that made me so callous. I do not know. After all, what was another death? I cared for her but I did not love her. Women never seem to understand the difference in the two things.

As to Lucy, Mary, and Frances, I did love each of them but after a short period of marriage, each in her own way became a burden. Each complained of the expenditures on horses and travel, and both Mary and Frances objected to my forays with my best friend. Oh, yes, they did, Holmes. It is one thing to say the words, 'Go with Mr Holmes, Dear.' It is another to receive the cold stares and animosity upon return. Lucy, of course, being the adventurous type always wanted to go along. The resentment came from being excluded.

As to their deaths, it was fairly easy. A handful of pepper in the eyes of Lucy's horse just before the gate did the trick. The horse could not see and was in agony. I knew well the course and of the deep donga on the other side.

Mary was a digitalis overdose made from the foxglove in her garden. Should things have gone wrong, I could not afford to be found with a missing supply from my surgery.

Frances only required a small cut, for there was no real infection but a large dose of strychnine on three successive days. The question might arise how she received the injury, so there had to be a public incident - hence, the carriage accident. I knew that, arriving at a hospital with a diagnosis and a plan of treatment, I would not be questioned. When you confronted me at Simpson's that night twenty one years ago, I knew my luck had run its course. That was something I never did figure out with the ponies.

In case you wondered Holmes, I really did love Martha. By then I had given up the horses and the gambling. I truly wanted to be with her. But I also knew I could not trust myself. When a woman became an inconvenience, she simply had to go and I loved Martha too much to take that chance.

Please know that I have always considered you my greatest friend and I leave this world being the better for having known you.

Your Friend,

John

Reaching into the match safe by the kettle arm he struck a match on the stove and lighted the letter. When it was well involved, he dropped it behind the logs. He then placed the tokens back in the box and placed the box on the mantle.

"Some tea, Mr Holmes?"

"Thank you, Mrs Hudson; I believe a cup would do well right now."

"What was the package, sir?"

"Ah, just some mementos from Dr Watson, I'm afraid he is gone."

"Poor man. Well, we all have to go I suppose." Her voice broke slightly at the words. "You go sit out on the porch and I'll bring your tea straight away."

Holmes watched her go back into the kitchen, then walked to his favourite chair on the porch and sat down. Ferdinand III came over and lay down next his master. The sun was already going down: it was indeed getting late. Holmes looked at the cliffs and the gulls. His eyes began to tear.

"I knew, Watson. I always knew."

Also from Kieran McMullen

Military Thrillers

Watson's Afghan Adventure

Sherlock Holmes and The Mystery of the Boer Wagon

Sherlock Holmes and The Irish Rebels

[and special hardback edition of all three novels 'Holmes and Watson: The War Years']

www.mxpublishing.com

Sherlock Holmes and Enoch Hale Series – co-written with Dan Andriacco

Sherlock Holmes and The Amateur Executioner

www.mxpublishing.com

Raising funds and awareness for
www.saveundershaw.com

The Many Watsons

www.mxpublishing.com

Also from Dan Andriacco

A series of modern murder-mysteries that all Sherlock Holmes fans will enjoy.

"No Police Like Holmes is an exciting and witty romp - not about Holmes but about his fans. The world's third-largest private collection of Sherlockiana has been donated to St Benignus, a small college in a small town in Ohio, and to celebrate, the college is hosting the Investigating Arthur Conan Doyle and Sherlock Holmes Colloquium. Jeff Cody, the college's PR director (and part-time crime writer), is an amused observer until the event is blighted by a real theft and a real murder, and he realises that there's rather a lot of suspects in deerstalkers. As if things weren't bad enough, Cody and his ex-girlfriend also become suspects."

The Sherlock Holmes Society of London

www.mxpublishing.com